GRAVE WATCH

SOUL READER SERIES BOOK THREE

ANNIE ANDERSON

GRAVE WATCH

ARCANE SOULS WORLD

Soul Reader Book 3

International Bestselling Author

Annie Anderson

Edited by Angela Sanders

Cover Design by Tattered Quill Designs

www.annieande.com

BOOKS BY ANNIE ANDERSON

THE ARCANE SOULS WORLD

GRAVE TALKER SERIES

Dead to Me

Dead & Gone

Dead Calm

Dead Shift

SOUL READER SERIES

Night Watch

Death Watch

Grave Watch

THE WRONG WITCH SERIES

Spells & Slip-ups

THE ETHEREAL WORLD

ROGUE ETHEREAL SERIES

Woman of Blood & Bone

Daughter of Souls & Silence

Lady of Madness & Moonlight

Sister of Embers & Echoes

Priestess of Storms & Stone

Queen of Fate & Fire

PHOENIX RISING SERIES

(Formerly the Ashes to Ashes Series)

Flame Kissed

Death Kissed

Fate Kissed

Shade Kissed

Sight Kissed

ROMANTIC SUSPENSE NOVELS

SHELTER ME SERIES

Seeking Sanctuary

Reaching Refuge

"I think you're my sister," the blonde blurted, her brilliant blue eyes pleading for me to believe her.

That wasn't the problem. I believed her—honestly, I did. Given what had transpired over the last few days, I'd pretty much believe anything at this point.

The actual problem was that not only did my long-lost, "totally a cop" sister show up on my doorstep after the biggest battle of my life, but she also brought a couple of ABI agents with her. I had a love-hate relationship with the Arcane Bureau of Investigation. The "love" because they paid the Night Watch boatloads of money to pick up their strays, and the "hate" because I was pretty sure that if they caught a whiff of what I'd been doing over the last year, my ass would be reduced to cannon fodder.

The agents, I knew.

The sister, I did not.

Not to mention, it was difficult to hold up a tough "I'm a badass, and I'll eat you for breakfast" air while being faced with the reality of my whole world being thrown on its ear. Truth be told, this wasn't the first time I had been tossed on my ass, but being confronted by a potentially *not*-evil sibling was on a whole other level.

The blonde—AKA, Detective Darby Adler—was a tall, slender woman in her mid-twenties, standing a few inches above my respectable five seven. Beside her was a tiny, dark-haired ABI agent that I'd met in passing. Agent Kenzari seemed nice enough, but it was the forbidding figure standing at their backs that gave me pause. Agent Bishop La Roux seemed to be contemplating my demise—especially if I replied in a way that he didn't like.

Well, he could try…

"Got to say, I wasn't expecting you to just show up here," I blurted, my mouth running off with the first thing that ran through my brain. After Azrael's parting words, I'd sort of hoped I wouldn't see hide nor hair of my siblings for a little while. What with our douchebag of a brother trying to kill me and all, the thought of a family reunion wasn't exactly on my to-do list. "In fact,

I wasn't expecting anyone to show up here. No offense, but the last time people made an unannounced visit, it turned into a bloodbath." A grimace yanked at my lips as the memory of that damn, blasted knife sailing end over end flashed in my brain.

I'd tried very hard over the last several hours to *not* think of that knife. Tried not to remember how it stuck in Bastian's side, his last gasps of breath. Yes, he was currently alive at the moment, but I got a sinking feeling in my gut whenever he was out of my sight. *Neurotic, party of one?*

"And that was yesterday," I tacked on for emphasis. It was not a good time for her to just be showing up on my doorstep.

Not. At. All.

"Oh, I like her." A voice broke in, startling me. It wasn't necessarily the Irish lilt, but more that the voice seemed to have come from what appeared to be an honest-to-god ghost. A no-shit, see-through, messenger from the other side, ghost.

Yes, I'm a walking, talking dead girl, but a ghost? No, thank you.

Was this a new thing I could do because I'd gone to the In-Between? Or was this something else?

My back hit the door in the middle of my scramble to get away, and instantly, I scolded myself. I'd latched onto evil souls in the In-Between with no problem, happy to send them to whatever Hell was waiting for them. But here? Now? I wasn't exactly sure. And that was only if I wasn't in the middle of a psychotic break or anything.

"Holy *shit*. Can you see Hildy?" Bishop asked, clearly aghast. "Is that a family trait or something?"

Family trait? That didn't sound good, but also if the ghost had a name, that likely meant I wasn't losing my freaking mind.

I swallowed hard, trying to get myself under control. "Hildy?"

The man hovered next to Darby, wearing something out of the nineteenth century. Blond curls swept from under a jaunty top hat, the royal-blue ribbon at the base matching his paisley cravat perfectly. His waistcoat was a beautiful, crushed velvet, but his outer jacket had to be some sort of thicker material. Wool, maybe. His eyes were the same crystalline blue as Darby's, only a little more transparent.

"Hildenbrand O'Shea," the ghost offered, moving to the head of the pack. "I'm Darby's grandfather. You can call me Hildy if you like. I kind of like that you can see me. It makes practical jokes a lot more fun." He muttered that last bit *sotto voce* like he fully intended on pulling a joke or five, and I was going to be in on it whether I liked it or not.

The nervous laugh that escaped my throat might have been mildly frantic, but that was neither here nor there. If Darby's eyes were anything to go by, I probably sounded a hell of a lot more hysterical than I'd intended. "You can see him, too?"

Darby shifted on her feet, an uncomfortable sort of shuffling that told me she wasn't exactly keen that this part of her life had been uncovered so quickly. "Yeah, I can see him all right. But not just him." She winced, tugging on the collar of her shirt. "I see all ghosts. It's why I make a good homicide detective. It's easier to solve murders with a little help from the inside."

A homicide detective who can see ghosts? That sounded like a match made in Heaven... or Hell. By how uncomfortable she was acting, I had a feeling it was more of the Hell variety, which I knew well enough.

Sister. I have a sister. And she seems... nice.

I couldn't say why that thought made me feel all warm in my middle, but it was something I wasn't too keen on investigating. A change of subject was in order.

"Well, since no one has screamed the house down that you're not allowed to be here, I figure it's probably cool to let you in." Relaxing, I grabbed the knob. "We're a weird bunch, but it's home, you know?"

I turned just in time to see Bishop wince.

"Yeah, about that," he muttered, scratching at his neck. "I *may* have knocked out your comms for a little bit. Didn't want anyone flambéing us before we even got an introduction. I'll remove my spell in just a second, promise."

He knocked out the comms? Like, did he just snap his fingers and turn all Harper's hard work into dust or something? "Ohh, Harper is going to kill you. Not really," I amended, grimacing. "I know threatening an ABI agent is probably frowned upon. Just…" I shook my head at the sheer stupidity falling out of my mouth. "Come on in."

But as I opened the door, a streak of white bone came racing out of the house. *Isis.* I'd never had a cat, but I'd had a family dog. Otis was a runner, too, always bolting from the house the first chance he got. But Isis wasn't Otis, and she wasn't exactly running far. Instead of bolting out into the night, the bone kitty leapt into Darby's arms and instantly began a rumble of a purr as she rubbed her head against Darby's jaw.

Why, that little traitor.

"Umm… that's Isis," I muttered, more than a little put out that she was just fawning all over my sister. It was funny when she did it to me because it annoyed the shit out of Simon. It was not cool when it was my turn. Rude. "I thought I was the only one she did that to. Must be Daddy's death juice."

Her face went a little green. "Death juice? Eww, that's just wrong. I do not need to think about our father's sperm, thank you."

That wasn't where I'd been going with that, but… "Okay, so maybe we'll get along just fine."

I couldn't help it—with the stress of the last few days, coupled with meeting my supposed long-lost sister —who could blame me? I dissolved into a snickering mess, bending double as my giggles turned into belly rocking laughter. Wiping tears from my eyes, I led the way into the living room, my mirth dying just as soon as it was borne, once I caught sight of the rather sizable bloodstain still marring the hardwood at the base of the stairs.

Every time I saw that stain, I heard Bastian's scream again. It was why I'd been cleaning it in the first place. Like if I could just get it up, I wouldn't hear that sound anymore. I wouldn't see that damn blade again. I wouldn't remember his shallow breaths as he…

Tearing my gaze from the stain, I tried not to let my whole body go cold. Tried to remember that he was okay and alive, and breathing and right upstairs talking to Emrys.

He's alive, Sloane. He's not going anywhere.

Blinking away the coming tears, I met Darby's gaze. "You okay?"

I shook myself, slapping on a false smile as I desperately tried to dispel the ache in my throat. "Fine. We were attacked yesterday. It was—"

"Who the fuck isn't warded in this house? I swear to Christ himself, ya'll better fix it now before I get angry," Harper screeched from the landing, cutting off my hasty explanation. It was just as well. "Honestly. Is it so hard?"

I stifled a laugh, announcing our company. "We have guests, Harper. Maybe take the rage down a notch?"

Like that was going to happen.

Harper's head peeked over the upstairs railing, surprise coloring her face before her eyes narrowed in suspicion as they locked unerringly onto Bishop. "Did you do something to my sensors?"

He gave her a sly grin that was anything but sorry. "Yes, but I'll put them back exactly as they were in just a moment. Care to alert Thomas that we're here?"

"He already knows," Thomas grumbled from the door to the dining room, his voice startling virtually everyone but me. I'd felt his presence long before he spoke, but I seemed to be the only one.

Thomas raked a hand through his black, shoulder-length hair, his pale jade eyes narrowing on Bishop.

"Wait a minute," Darby muttered, her blue eyes going wide. "Thomas? Ingrid's Thomas?"

She knew Ingrid? My respect for my newfound sister shot up about a thousand degrees.

"I take it you're Darby Adler. I can't thank you enough for coming to her aid. I hate to think that I would have lost her had you not."

So, she not only knew my tiny vampire friend, but she'd also saved her ass? Okay, I was now convinced.

"I didn't do it alone," she muttered, tilting her head in Bishop and Sarina's direction as she tugged on her collar again.

"Wait," Harper broke in, "you guys are the crew that helped the Dubois nest? You realize keeping them alive is the only reason we're alive today. We were getting our asses kicked before they swooped in."

Darby's face went white as she wobbled on her feet. Slowly, she rested her hands on her knees as she sucked in deep breaths, tears swimming her eyes as she did her best to calm down. It mirrored my own internal turmoil so much my heart damn near disintegrated in my chest.

I knelt at her feet, the urge to comfort her insurmountable. "Hey, it's okay. We're okay."

"No, it isn't." She gave me a watery chuckle as she swiped at her cheeks. "It's not okay, and we're not okay. Admitting that isn't weakness, little sister."

I could only blink at the "little sister" comment. "It's weird that that felt good, right? I shouldn't like that at all, but I really do."

And I did. I really, really did. The Night Watch was family—something I hadn't had in a long time. But Darby felt different. More. Like I'd lost a piece of myself, and now it was found.

"How do you feel about familial hugs? My dad— the man who raised me—is pretty big on them. Considering he's my only stable parent, I'd like to pass that on."

What the hell could I say to that? My family had been the same—happy, together, full of hugs and forehead kisses, and family meals. It was like getting a piece of them back. "I could go for that."

She wasted no time, launching herself at me and attack-hugged me with precisely zero regard to decorum. Her grip wasn't just tight, either. It was on a whole other level of strength that made me rethink her fragility.

"I know I'm dead and all, but choking me until I

pass out is still pretty uncomfortable," I croaked, and Darby pulled away so fast she nearly dumped me on my ass.

"What?" she barked, her voice cracking like a whip of cop-voice mixed with big sister mixed with mama bear. "Explain. Now."

Confused, I righted myself. "I—I thought you knew. I figured Azrael would have told you since he sent you here."

"He didn't," she said, shaking her head. "Send us, I mean." She jerked her chin at Sarina. "*She* found you. *She* brought me here. Azrael hasn't told me dick. Not even your name before yesterday, and he sure as shit didn't mention that you were... *Dead?* Like really dead or like *un*dead? Because I've never heard of a dead girl just walking around all calm like. I mean, Hildy does it, but..." She whipped her head to the man it seemed only we alone could see. "How do you do that, by the way?"

"Who is she talking to?" Thomas asked, his approach slow and methodical as if he were assessing my sister for brain damage.

Darby's cheeks went pink, her gaze falling to her feet as she realized her mistake. I couldn't imagine being able to see ghosts all the time. Were they every-where? Did they know she could see them? And was this my fate, too, talking to people no one else could see?

"Her grandfather," Bishop answered, shooting a withering glare at Thomas. "Darby can see and speak to the dead."

Thomas gave me a look of concern before slowly nodding his head.

"I have a couple of other tricks up my sleeve, too," Darby muttered, raising her chin but refusing to look anyone in the eye. *Dammit.*

"The night I became this?" I began. "I died. Azrael tried to bring me back, but I'd been gone too long, so…" I trailed off, not knowing if my story would make her feel any less like a freak. We did share a gene pool, after all.

"He gave you a piece of himself," she guessed. "He brought you back the hard way rather than let you rest."

On the one hand, Darby didn't seem uncomfortable anymore. On the other, she was lighting up like a Roman candle on the Fourth of July. A white light started at the center of her chest, flowing down her arms and pooling in a blinding concentration of power that made her whole body practically vibrate.

"Umm…" I chuckled nervously, staring at the hand

still latched onto my shoulder. "Did you know your hands glow a little when you're mad?"

She yanked her hands back, her sheepish expression returning full force. "Sorry. I was just mentally berating our sperm donor for being an absolute fuck stick. I'll try to keep my shit under control."

Somehow, I doubted that was even in the realm of possibilities, but whatever.

"I like her," Harper called from upstairs. "She can stay and don't bother with the ward. If she's anything like Sloane, she'd burn through it, anyway."

Darby shot me a look. "Ward?"

I shook my head at Harper's antics as I dropped an arm around my sister's waist. "Harper's an empath, so emotions are kind of a problem for her. We try to be respectful and ward ourselves, but evidently, our lineage is kind of a bitch on that front."

And that was putting it lightly.

I had a feeling my sister knew exactly what I was talking about.

2

Leading my sister and her ABI cronies upstairs, I felt a sick pit of dread yawn wide in my belly. Sure, it was one thing to meet a sibling, but it was quite another to introduce said sister to the man you were in love with. Not to mention, I was sort of concerned about just leading two ABI agents through the house.

"It's going to be fine, Sloane," Thomas muttered so no one but me could hear, likely hearing my stupid heart beating out of my chest. "I already texted Emrys to let her know. She's waiting for us."

I couldn't say Thomas' pronouncement was the comforting assurance he'd meant it to be, but I marched up the stairs, anyway. At the landing, Harper stood with her arms crossed, eyeing our visitors with her patented skepticism. Well, until Sarina skirted around us all and approached our resident empath.

Harper squinted her eyes as she assessed the agent. "Psychic?" she guessed, tilting her head to the side.

Sarina mirrored her, tilting her head in the same direction as if it would ease the empath's mind. "Oracle."

At the correction, Harper simply shrugged and held out a hand to shake. "Good to meet you."

I wasn't shocked at Harper's quick acquiescence. No, what shocked the shit out of me was the ease at which she held out her hand. I distinctly recalled Harper's aversion to touch. In fact, out of respect, I refused to touch her unless she initiated it for fear of hurting her. Sarina had no such compunction, and as soon as the agent's hand slid into the empath's, a smile dawned on Harper's face that actually hurt my heart, it was so beautiful. I didn't think Harper did that very often—or at least not that I'd seen—and it made me mad and sad all at the same time.

"What the fuck, Harper?" I growled before I thought better of it, my hands almost reaching to touch her but pulling back before I made contact.

Harper's gaze broke with Sarina's, her grin brightening like the coming morning. "I should have done this before. Maybe if I would have done it with Celeste, then none of this would have happened."

A slight wrinkle marred the happiness on her face and pissed me off. "That is not your fault, and you know it."

It made me sick to think that Harper blamed herself for Celeste's actions. None of it had been her fault. It hadn't been any of our faults.

"Someone explain what is going on, please," Bishop barked, hovering at his partner's back like he'd snatch her away at any second.

Sarina gave him a quelling expression before directing her attention back to Harper. "Harper reads emotions naturally through the ambient air, but when she touches someone, she can read nearly every thought, every emotion, everything, and the longer she touches you, the more she can see. Since I'm sort of like her, it isn't as bad as if she were to read another person. Plus, since I'm in the know about all the things, she only has to read me and not the whole group."

"Yeah, but I can't read the future like you can," Harper countered ruefully. "That would have saved my bacon a time or two."

Sarina shrugged. "It has its moments. None that I'd wish on anyone, though."

"Ain't that the truth," Harper muttered, shifting her

eyes to Bishop. "You turn my shit on again or what? Given the environment, leaving us unprotected isn't exactly a good thing."

Bishop winced apologetically as he rubbed the back of his neck. "Already done, but do a check to be safe. If you need help beefing up the wards, I'd be happy to lend a hand, too."

I could practically hear Thomas roll his eyes. "Sure, we'd love an ABI agent just moseying on through our security system. No problem."

Bishop's expression turned wounded. "What makes you think after all these years that I would do a fucked-up thing like that? I thought we were friends."

Thomas' eyes went red as needle-like fangs peeked out from under his lips. "Is that what you'd call it?"

"Okay, gentlemen," I growled, sending a steely-eyed glare at Thomas, "let's keep our cool here."

"Yes," Darby agreed, elbowing Bishop in the ribs. "Let's. I don't know how you feel about the ABI, but I'm not a fan." She looked at Bishop and Sarina, giving them a sheepish shrug. "No offense. But my mother runs the Knoxville branch, and well… She's dirty. Like up to her eyeballs in bullshit, sent me to prison for almost a year, body-snatching, baby-killing, *dir-ty*. She's in the middle of this shit, and I'll be damned if she tries a fucking thing on you, so…" Darby shook her head, pinching a brow. "If you need help, I got you. You need backup, I'm down. You need me to bury a body, I know a guy."

I couldn't help the snort that escaped me. "His name wouldn't happen to be Gerry, would it?"

Gerry had been a mighty fine ally once upon a time —you know, before he tattled on me to the Night Watch. I had buried many a body in his cemetery, and all it cost me was a few cases of whiskey. It was the tattling thing that really got to me, though.

Darby blinked at me, clearly stunned. "You know Gerry? How is the old bastard?"

I thought about him being pissed that Booth was in pieces all over his graveyard. "Cantankerous as ever. I can't believe you know the guy that…" I trailed off, shaking myself. *No need to confess your murders to the cop, Sloane. Shut up for once in your life, will you?* "Never mind."

"So, you're a police officer who offers to bury bodies for her little sister? And that doesn't make you dirty, *how again?*" Thomas asked, his jaw clenched as if he were trying to cause a damn scene.

I was about to give him a piece of my mind when Darby beat me to it. "Who says the bodies we'd be burying would be human?" she asked, coyly tilting her head to the side. "I don't police the arcane, but if you don't believe me, why don't you call Ingrid or Mags. They'll vouch for me."

"Mags?" Thomas' face went absolutely ashen as he sputtered, "The vampire queen of Knoxville lets you call her *Mags*?"

Darby waggled her eyebrows at him as her smile turned sinister. "That she does. She owes me. Lots. But that's neither here nor there. Now, weren't we up here to meet someone?"

At her prompting, I pushed through the group, giving Thomas an extra special shove so he knew I was more than a little pissed at him. I got that he was being protective, but did he need to be an asshole about it?

Three quick raps of my knuckles, and Bastian swung the door wide. It was almost as if he'd been standing on the other side of it, just waiting for me to knock. Dark hair and blazing bottle-green eyes capped a mammoth frame that screamed violence, but all I saw was the way his eyes warmed when they latched onto me. Instantly, I felt like I could breathe again as the weight of worry slid from my chest.

"What's this, love?"

Bastian's quiet rumble was like a warm blanket and a hot drink on a cold day. It was comfort and reassurance. I almost teared up, wanting to tell him everything, but instead, I rolled up on my toes and pressed a kiss to his lips. "I'll tell you in a minute. This is a story only to be told once. Can you get the gang for me? I promise not to start the tale until you come back?"

He narrowed his beautiful eyes at me, but that didn't stop a trace of a smile from pulling at the corner of his mouth. "As you wish, love."

A few minutes later, the lot of us were assembled in Emrys' office, and I started the meeting with a bang. "Okay, everyone, I'd like you to meet Darby Adler. My sister." That last bit felt odd coming out of my mouth, but good all at the same time. "With her, is Agent Bishop La Roux and Sarina Kenzari with the ABI. And there is also a ghost you can't see named Hildy."

Clem gave Darby's ghostly grandfather a finger wave. "Oh, I can see him. How's it going, handsome?"

"Holy Jesus, Mary, and Joseph," Hildy said under his breath, having the good sense to blush, as he pulled at his cravat and eyed our resident revenant with interest.

I made the introductions, but I was sort of at a loss. Though Emrys had no such troubles. "Can I ask why you're here? It's not often we have ABI agents traipsing through our home. Are ya here in an official capacity?"

Bishop shot a look at Darby and answered, "Absolutely not. As far as the ABI is concerned, we're not here, have never been here, and don't know you except in passing because of bounties. As far as anyone knows, we don't know you."

It was tough to know how to take that, and I wasn't the only one.

"Is that right?" Emrys replied, her odd reddish eyes flashing in affront.

Bishop put himself in front of Darby, practically shielding her with his body. "The ABI was breached three days ago. Agents I'd known for years slaughtered. At the same time, there was a prison break. I know my director is involved. She..." Bishop shook his head, hesitating to say the last bit.

"She's my mother," Darby finished his sentence. "Mariana O'Shea is my mother, and she has infiltrated the Knoxville coven. That's not why I'm here, but I figure this is a two-birds-one-stone kind of deal. I came here to meet my sister. My friends are here to ask for your help."

Darby's expression seemed wounded for a single, solitary moment before she wiped it clean. Like she hadn't realized the agents' plans until just that moment.

Oh. Ouch.

I didn't know what to think about Bishop La Roux, but I sort of sensed that he and Darby were a thing. However, if these two were a thing, he was about to be in the doghouse for the foreseeable future.

"I kind of figured our father would have sent you, but I guess not." I shrugged, trying to get her mind off her douchey maybe-boyfriend. "Hey, speaking of, does the name Essex Drake mean anything to you?" She shook her head, and I snorted. "Well, hold onto your ass. We have a brother, goes by the name X."

"Oh, I know about him. Bastard murderer with a penchant for killing siblings?" she asked to confirm.

"That's the one. Well, Azrael told me to pass along some information. This X? Well, his real name is Essex."

Then that pit of dread I'd been feeling? Well, it decided to turn into a full-on canyon.

Darby turned to Bishop, opening her mouth to tell him something before her eyes narrowed and she snapped it shut. A realization must have dawned, and she gritted her teeth, her hand shining like Christmas morning.

Written all over Bishop was a fair amount of guilt on top of shame.

He'd already known.

And now my sister was pissed.

"You're glowing again," I remarked, and oh, so slowly, she peeled her gaze from Bishop and locked those betrayed eyes on me. I couldn't tell what was going on in her head, but if I had a guess, she was contemplating shooting Bishop in the kneecaps or tossing him off a cliff.

"Did Azrael give you any other details?" she croaked, her eyes filling with awful tears.

I swallowed hard, trying not to snap her dumb boyfriend's neck. That was a thing sisters did for each other, right? "No, just that he was sorry he didn't tell you sooner."

She nodded like I'd said something profound, clearly trying to get herself under control. By the glowing hands, she wasn't doing such a good job.

"I know who he is," Bishop murmured, and the whole room went wired.

"Son, I don't know you," Axel began, his thick Texan drawl doing nothing to conceal the threat in it, "but I'm gonna need you to be real specific on how you know this man and who he is to you."

Bishop skirted one of the chairs in front of Emrys' desk and plopped onto it like he had a right. "He's the second in command at headquarters in a position called 'The Overseer.' He's my boss's boss."

Darby stared at Bishop in silence for a few long moments before she pivoted on a heel and flew from the room, taking her glowing hands and bottled-up rage with her. Hildy whisked after her, shooting a murderous glare at the betraying agent. Bishop followed, taking his life in his own hands as he raced after her like an idiot. I was tempted to trail behind them, but a warm hand on my shoulder stopped me.

"Let them hash it out, love," Bastian murmured in my ear. "We'll worry about burying his body later."

I snorted, wondering if old Gerry had a thing against me burying ABI agents.

"She won't kill him." Sarina sighed, plopping on the chair Bishop had just vacated. "Maim him, sure, but kill? Doubtful. She loves him too much."

I scoffed. *My sister loves that shmuck? Yeesh.*

A faint trace of a smile flitted across Sarina's lips as if she could read my mind. "He only found out a few days ago that they were one and the same," Sarina replied to my derision. "Since then, it's been a little hectic—what, with her almost getting killed about a zillion or so times. I swear that girl is going to give me an ulcer."

That reminded me of an offhanded comment that

Harper had made. Darby and Bishop had come to the Dubois nest's rescue, and to hear Thomas tell it, the attack had been vicious.

"Honestly, I don't know how she's still standing with what her mother has been doing," she said, a gust of a sigh following the words as she pinched the bridge of her nose. The scent of her worry filled my nostrils, making me seriously reconsider following my sister. "The level of cloaking that woman has is atrocious. Hiding from me is not an easy feat, and she's doing it without so much as a hitch."

Emrys sat back in her chair, her silence a tangible thing. "You said the director was her mother? You're telling me Mariana O'Shea is Darby's mum? I didn't think that woman was capable of mothering a child, let alone being unselfish enough to produce one in the first place."

"Tell us how you really feel, Emrys. Sheesh," Simon muttered, wincing.

"You've been lucky enough to avoid her thus far, my boy. Trust me. If she'd been in charge when you'd been arrested, you wouldn't be here today. Or you'd be in her pocket doing her bidding just to stay alive."

Sarina nodded, the stark resignation on her face a testament to Emrys' words.

"We're going to need extra protection around the

house if we're going against that wretch. Maybe a bloody moat if need be. I never thought I'd see the day," she muttered, shaking her head.

That was not at all a comforting statement, and knowing Emrys, she didn't exaggerate.

This was about to get so much worse.

3

When I woke up this afternoon, I didn't think I'd end up worried out of my mind about another person in my life. Considering the last three days, I kind of figured I'd be topped up on things to be frightened out of my mind about, but there I freaking was.

Swallowing back bile, I stared at the blood coming out of my sister's nose as she wilted in her man's arms. I was still on the fence about Bishop La Roux. It didn't really matter to me whether or not my sister had a thing for the tall death mage—what mattered was his penchant for keeping secrets. But the stark fear on his face and the way he clutched her to him had me tilting a bit.

After Darby stormed out of the room with Bishop

in tow, things had gone into hyperdrive. Bastian, Simon, and Dahlia worked together to beef up the warding around the property. Emrys made several phone calls, and what did I do?

I worried.

Well, that and try to contact my bitch-ass father to no avail.

Closing my eyes, I tried to picture him in my mind, tried to call to him.

Come on, Azrael. Just tell us what's going on. Tell us what we're supposed to do. You can't want to follow the rules so bad that you'd...

I was about to say that he couldn't want to follow the rules so bad that he'd let us die, but given his history, that was precisely what he'd do.

You want me to take your throne or whatever, right? How am I supposed to do that if my bitch-ass brother burns my life to the ground? Again.

Since giving answers wasn't in Azrael's wheelhouse, all I got was silence.

A silence that was broken when Harper yelled, "Incoming" from her open office door. "It's Bishop and Darby, and there is an injured girl with them."

But Harper didn't have to tell me. As soon as she said the words, I knew exactly what that feeling was.

"Axel, get ready," I hissed at the big man. "The girl is bad off."

I didn't know how I knew it. Didn't know how I translated the dreadful, twisted feeling in my gut into imminent death, but I did. It was the same feeling I'd gotten the moment before Simon and Dahlia died. The exact drop before Bastian had gotten a knife in his chest.

Axel sprang into action, whipping the door open about a millisecond after a dreadful pounding hammered the wood. I barely caught a glimpse of Axel and Darby. My gaze was trained on the battered girl in Bishop's arms as I stood rooted to the spot. I lost sight of them as they headed for the med bay, their retreating backs there and gone as they raced down the steps of the hidden entryway to the lower level. Not a moment later, Bishop reappeared, yelling for Thomas and Dahlia.

He was shouting—had to be. The veins on the side of his neck were bulging, and his face was a mix of pissed off and scared out of his mind, but I could barely hear him. In fact, he sounded like he was under-water. Then he was gone again, slipping back down from where he came.

And me?

I just stood there, the aching truth filling me with a terrible knowledge.

All I could feel was the coming death, but it wasn't at the end of my blade or my fangs, and this little girl didn't deserve it. Worse? Something was stirring in the direction of the med bay that wasn't from the girl at all. No, it had a very different signature. It was like a buzzing that was slowing down, but I hadn't noticed it before. Only once it began to fade did I realize what it was.

That buzz was Darby—Darby's life force or soul or whatever—and it was going quiet. I wanted to howl, wanted to race downstairs, and stop whatever it was that was diminishing her, but I was rooted, stuck. Unable to make my feet do anything but stay right where they were. Thomas and Dahlia hoofed it down the grand staircase, heading for the hidden one leading to the med bay, but before they could traverse those slippery stone steps, Bishop shoved through the door.

And in his arms was my sister, her skin like death, papery and pale. One arm hung limply at her side while the other lay draped over Bishop's shoulder. Bishop's jaw was granite as he carried her to the closest couch, the scent of Darby's blood high on the air.

"What happened to her?" I demanded, my question echoed by the transparent Hildy, who seemed to have popped in from nowhere.

"I'm fine," she insisted as she hung like a wet noodle in Bishop's arms. "Just tired is all."

Tired my ass. She was half-dead, and we both knew it. Hell, Hildy, Bishop, and anyone with a brain in their skull could see it. Did she think I was blind or something? "You know I can smell blood, right? And I have eyes. That hasn't escaped your attention at this point, has it?"

Bishop set her down on a plush couch, and she pried her eyes open with what seemed like a sheer force of will.

"No—though, the blood thing is new," she croaked, cracking a smile. Like that was going to put a Band-Aid on this bullshit. "I'll be fine. Faster if you have any ghosts lying around."

My gaze invariably went to Hildy, and he met it with a roll of his eyes.

"Oh, for fuck's sake," Hildy griped. "This is a damn disgrace. How much of your power did Azrael siphon off of ya, lass? The whole lot? Fucking bastard and his fucking rules. If he had a brain in his head, he'd leave ya with enough to spare, what with you runnin' head-long into danger as ya are." I hadn't noticed before, but Hildy had a thin cane in his hand, the handle a silver skull with emeralds for eyes. And those eyes began to glow, the magic lighting it up in a familiar way, almost like Isis' animated gaze.

Darby held up her hand. "Stop. I'm fine. Don't drain yourself too much."

He didn't answer her, but the glow to his cane grew brighter.

"Quit it. I said I was fine," she hissed, shoving herself off the couch like it took every ounce of her strength to do it.

"Well, at least you're on your feet then," Hildy hissed back, his top hat and cane winking out of sight.

"Okay, what the hell was that?" Bastian grumbled, staring my sister down like she was in serious need of a one-way ticket to a sanitorium. "First, you're pissed, running off to who knows where, then you two come back with a damn near dead girl in tow. Then you heal said girl, but that makes you sick, and now you're talking to people who aren't there? Am I getting this right?"

Simon sighed and rolled his eyes. "You know what grave talkers are, Bastian. Stop being a twat just because you can't see him."

"For fuck's sake," Hildy muttered, snapping his fingers. In an instant, Hildy went from slightly transparent to fully solid as he pierced Bastian with a perturbed glare. "Listen to your brother, mage."

Bastian uncrossed his arms, smiling at the now-solid ghost. "Hildenbrand O'Shea, you dead bastard. How have you been?"

Hildy shrugged. "Oh, you know, just trying to keep my granddaughter alive and my daughter from becoming a blight on the family name. You know, the usual."

"You call the most venerated grave talker in the known histories Hildy?" Simon said, aghast at the audacity of my older sister. "And he lets you?"

She turned to the man in question. "I'm going to need you to spill on all the grave talker deets. Every time people find out who you are, they freak the fuck out. It's weird."

"All in good time, lass. All in good time."

It sounded like a "never" if I ever heard one.

I heard Thomas' footsteps before the hidden door creaked once again. Thomas emerged, the rage blooming on his face a palpable thing. His gaze was trained right on Darby, too, which didn't make a lick of sense. "I'm going to need you to come with me, please. Alone."

"I don't think so," Bishop countered, squaring off against the ancient vampire like an idiot. I didn't know how old Thomas was, but I knew enough not to fight him if I wanted to keep all my limbs attached.

Dahlia slipped from the hidden doorway as well, her expression pinched with fury. "I want to know what happened to that girl, and I want to know now."

Dahlia's voice had always been quiet, always calm. Like getting riled was beneath her somehow. But this cold, ferocity had even me shaking in my boots. I liked it even less trained on my sister, which didn't make sense. I'd only known Darby a handful of hours, but she already felt like family.

She felt like home.

And that home was being threatened.

"We found her on our way back, crumpled up in a heap right outside the ward," Darby insisted, shaking her head. "I don't think I've ever seen her before today."

"Then why is that child saying your name? Why is she calling for you?" Dahlia hissed, her whole body practically vibrating with rage.

I had to admit that those were some outstanding questions—ones I couldn't even begin to answer.

"No good deed goes unpunished," Bishop muttered. "Fine. We're all going down there. I won't go in the bay, but I'll be damned if you think I'm letting you take my woman off to some underground lair just so you can accuse her of that bullshit. Not just no, but hell no."

I hadn't yet decided how I felt about Bishop La Roux, but I really appreciated how he was protecting my sister right about now—even if it was against people I trusted with my life.

"Works for me," Thomas said, gesturing to the doorway that led to Axel's domain.

Bishop tensed, gently pulling my sister behind him as he headed for the passage. And me? Well, I still couldn't make myself move from the spot I'd been cemented to for the last five minutes.

I tried my very hardest *not* to go down the slippery stone steps to the medical bay if I didn't have to. One, because being that far below ground gave me the willies, and two? Aunt Julie was still down there, her expired shell moldering in a body bag in Axel's freezer. Given that Axel was a ghoul, I tried *extremely* hard to not examine why he needed a freezer in the first place. With all that had happened over the last few months, I still hadn't seen to her body, nor had I really mourned the woman who had been like a second mother to me.

"You don't have to go down there, you know," Bastian whispered in my ear as he wrapped a comforting arm around my middle. I'd been so deep in my thoughts that I hadn't even heard him approach.

"No one would even look at you funny. You don't have to be the strong one all the time, love."

I huffed out a mirthless laugh and tilted my head back to shoot him a look. "Would you let Simon go down there alone, knowing he could be potentially attacked?"

Bastian let out a dark chuckle. "I would pity whatever poor fool decided to choose death, but I see your point. Though, I don't see how you've forged this bond so quickly. If I didn't know better, I'd think she'd spelled you."

His thoughts echoed my own, but I couldn't give him a reason why I wanted to protect a woman I'd just met any more than I could rationalize how I knew Dahlia was an ally or that Booth was a flaming danger turd. I just *knew*.

"I can't explain. It's just... she feels like home, you know?"

Bastian pressed his lips together, his brow wrinkling as he studied my face.

"She isn't like him," I insisted, referring to my murderous bastard of a brother. It almost made me gag every time I thought of Essex Drake as my brother. It made me want to rage, and burn things down, and scratch my own skin off.

Because his blood ran through me, too.

Surprise colored Bastian's expression before he locked it down. "I know that, love."

It was then that I realized that tears were gathering in my eyes. Why, I couldn't say, but there they were. "She isn't."

"I can tell you believe that, but there is a darkness in her, too. I know you can see it just like I can. The wrong pressure and she could easily turn to an awful path if she's not careful. Just like you could have but didn't."

Befuddled, I bleated out a shocked laugh. "You don't call over four hundred kills in a year an awful path? I'd hate to see what you think that is then."

Bastian's smile was smug as he pulled me around to face him. "Have you ever killed an innocent person?"

I flipped through my mental Rolodex of kills, full well knowing the answer. "No."

"Have you endangered the lives of good people, let them be slaughtered out of sheer indifference?"

Now I was getting irritated. "Of course not."

"Have you let murderers and rapists and abusers go free to inflict their poison onto their next victim?"

I gnashed my teeth. "You know the answer to that."

His green eyes practically glowed with mirth as he asked his next question. "Then how is your path an awful one, love?"

It really sucked having a wise, older-than-dirt mage as a boyfriend sometimes. How could I compete with half a millennium of experience and life lessons? Fun fact: I totally could not. Rather than tell him he was right, I rolled my eyes. Unerringly, they still found the door that everyone else had easily passed through.

"I don't know what to do about Julie's body," I admitted, my throat burning. "We never talked about what she wanted, and everything I can think of feels disrespectful. And the longer I wait, the more it hurts to do anything at all."

And what did I know about it, anyway? Julie had likely been the one to arrange everything when my parents died. How had she done it all on her own? I didn't have the first clue of where to start, and that made me feel guilty and mad and...

"We'll figure it out, love."

It was the gentle care in his voice that did me in, and I let three tears fall before I sucked in a huge breath.

"You don't have to go down there. You and I can just stay here."

Nodding, I watched the door, praying nothing went wrong down there.

4

It turned out that I had no need to worry. Five minutes after the whole of the house—save for me and Bastian—traipsed down to Axel's lair, the lot of them stomped right back up the steps. Bishop led the way, cradling the young girl in his arms like he thought she might break. Behind him were Darby and Dahlia—both of their faces pinched like they'd seen some shit and were definitely not happy about it.

Bishop set the girl down on the couch much like he had done with Darby earlier, only his expression was three beats past haunted. Something had gone down in that med bay—I had no doubt in my mind. The scent of cold sweat and dried blood and still-healing injuries permeated the living room, the source the beaten preteen who was now being covered with a soft blanket by the odd ABI agent. Bishop's fingers curled into fists as he stared at the sleeping child, and if I hadn't peeked at his face, I wouldn't have known he wasn't a millisecond from killing the kid.

"You guys have a gym in this place?" he croaked, his gaze never wavering from the couch.

I squeezed Bastian's hand and lifted my chin in the direction of the training room. Bastian dropped a kiss to my temple and skirted past me. "Sure, mate. It's this way," he said, clapping the agent on his shoulder. "Let's go blow things up and pretend the world isn't shite, yeah?"

Hesitantly, Bishop nodded, letting himself be led away, his fingers still balled into fists. One look at the girl on the couch, and I could see why he was so pissed.

"I thought you healed her?" I blurted, taking in the kid's bruises and swollen features. This was someone's baby, and she'd been shoved to the brink of death.

Darby shook her head. "I don't have enough juice to heal her all the way. I only kept her from dying."

Shock stole my breath as her words filtered through my brain. Ungracefully, I plopped onto one of the club chairs, my gaze trained on the small lump on the couch. Darby had given this child what little life she'd had to spare, damn near killing herself in the process. I wanted to scold her, but I knew enough about myself to know I would have done the same damn thing in her shoes. As admirable as it probably was on the outside, I was really starting to hate the family martyr complex.

A lot.

We sat in silence for a while until Dahlia got a wild hair up her ass, starting an inquisition that didn't need to happen right this second. "Why was she calling for you?" she asked, tapping her bottom lip as she examined Darby with her penetrating stare. "It doesn't make any sense. She doesn't know you, right?"

Darby shook her head. "Not that I know of. Axel said she smelled of witch, but sniffing out witches isn't exactly in my wheelhouse, so…"

Dahlia tapped at her lip again, staring off into the distance. "Would it be unethical for me to take a blood sample at this point?"

I rolled my eyes so hard I thought they were going to roll on out of my head. "From a child? Dude, you know better."

Dahlia flicked a trio of braids off her shoulder and sighed. "Yeah, I do. I just want to know who she is. I feel like I should know her, and I don't, and it's bugging the crap out of me." She chewed on her bottom lip in deliberation before jumping out of her seat. "I've got it!"

Then she took off down the stairs without so much as a nod toward an explanation.

"I love that girl, but what the fuck?" I muttered, shaking my head.

Dahlia was usually so levelheaded, it freaked me out a little to have her so out of sorts. But everything was out of sorts, wasn't it? Buildings getting raided, ABI agents getting murdered. Prisoners escaping. Attacks on vampire nests. Nothing made sense anymore—not that it ever really did.

"You say that your mom is the ABI director here?" I asked, wondering how deep in the hole the ABI really was. Darby had said her mother was dirty. If that was true, what chance did we have?

She kept her gaze on the child as she answered. "Sort of?" she said with a bit of a hand waggle. "You know the ABI was attacked a few days ago, right?"

Oh, I knew. The last week had been bounties, explosions, and attacks galore. "Of course. We had to round up the fugitives from the prison break. I've never slept so little in my life." I pinched the bridge of my nose, remembering the water tower incident, followed by the stupid graveyard extravaganza of bullshit. "Then I got blown up. It was a whole mess."

Darby's jaw dropped. "I'm sorry, what?"

"Oh, yeah. So, remember I'm technically dead?" *Great lead-in, Sloane. That won't freak her out.* "Well, I can't exactly die because I'm dead already. So, no worries there, but our brother has—or had—a…" I paused, attempting to explain the last twenty-four hours. "Okay, I don't know exactly who they were to each other. Partner, maybe? Anyway, he had this partner named Celeste, who was this gifted syphoner witch, and she did a number on me. She was also basically a Trojan horse kind of deal and damn near got everyone killed, which is why Harper is freaked you breached the system." I winced again. "Actually, full transparency?" And I had to be really clear here because there was shit she needed to know. Stuff that could change things.

She blinked at me like I was a Martian or something. "Uh, yeah?"

"Technically, a few of us did die," I admitted, pitching my voice low, "but I brought them back?"

She frowned, her brow pulling together in confusion. "What, like a death mage?"

I stuck out my bottom lip, shaking my head. "Not exactly?"

Darby leveled me with a maternal eyebrow raise, coupled with a slight narrowing to her eyes that meant business. "Why are you saying it like a question? Do you not know? Or do you just not want to tell me?"

If we had actually grown up together, I would have been mincemeat with that look. No wonder she was such a good detective. I couldn't help but blurt everything out. "I went to the In-Between and brought them back."

She shifted in her seat, blinking at me. She did that a lot. Though, I did just spill the beans about a completely different dimension, coupled with the fact that I'd single-handedly brought three people back to life. At once. Given the way that Simon kept staring at me like I was the damn boogeyman, well, it wasn't hard to guess that this wasn't anywhere in the realm of normal.

At her continued gaping silence, I continued my blurting, "It's where ghosts live, I think, before they move on. Azrael wasn't exactly forthcoming on the details, but that's what I figure it is. But there's only so much time you can stay there before you get stuck. Simon, Dahlia, and Bastian died, and I..."

"You brought them back," she whispered, finishing my sentence.

Nodding, I dropped my gaze to the twisted fingers on my lap. "I sort of got stuck there, too, but Azrael got me back out. That's when he told me to let you know who our brother is. I think he told me because he knew you were coming. And I think he knows something is coming for us. *He* is coming for us. I think Azrael wanted us to be prepared."

She growled softly under her breath. "It would be nice if he just fucking told us instead of being so goddamn cryptic. It's tough to gauge what's coming if we don't know the whole story. I mean, given what I've gleaned already, this whole thing is a tangle of vines— only the vines are snakes, and the snakes are venomous."

Well, she isn't wrong.

Racing steps sounded before Dahlia emerged from the med bay with a wad of bloody gauze in her fist.

"What in the—" Darby muttered only to be cut off by Dahlia's crow of triumph.

"I found some non-creepily sourced blood," she crowed, as if that wasn't the weirdest fucking thing she could have said. "I need to find this girl's people— either to return her to her home or beat someone's ass, I don't know which."

A small part of me figured it was the latter more than the former, but what did I know?

Dahlia made a beeline for the circular entryway table, hauling the large vase of flowers off of it. In a matter of moments, there was a purple cloth covering the wood and a gleaming metal bowl in the center.

"What are you doing?" Axel drawled, his head peeking over the banister as he watched Dahlia assemble the ingredients for what I hoped was a location spell of epic proportions.

Dahlia shot him a sly grin that would put a damn demon to shame. "I'm finding the truth. It's better than eating food, sitting on my ass, or pretending to train."

I couldn't help the offended "Hey" that came out of my mouth.

"Don't like my assessment?" My small witchy friend shrugged. "Fine. But I'm not letting a child just sit here without looking for her people."

Then she dropped the gauze in the bowl, along with a slew of other ingredients, and lit the whole lot on fire with a snap of her fingers. A moment later, she extinguished the flames with another snap before pouring the still-burning remains on the tabletop. Curiosity got the better of me, and I peeled myself from my seat to inspect further. Darby must have had the same idea because we paced together to watch what appeared to be a map curl up into smoldering ash.

I didn't know what the remaining bits of paper meant, but Darby did.

"Poppy's a St. James witch," she muttered more to herself than anyone else.

I could only assume the little girl was Poppy, but I didn't understand the significance of being a St. James witch—not really. Shifting to the side, my gaze met frightened brown ones.

"You're not going to send me back there, are you?" Poppy whispered, ducking her nose beneath the top of the couch like she'd hide from us at the first sign of danger.

I knew the answer to that question without so much as a glance at anyone else. There was no way I'd be handing her over to anyone without a thorough background check and probably a teensy taste of their blood for good measure.

No way in hell.

"If your coven did that to you," my sister growled, blind rage leaking out of her iron control, "then absolutely not. I don't give a shit what anyone says." Then she winced, shooting a defiant look at Dahlia. "No offense."

"None taken," she replied, waving away Darby's words as she pulled her braids into a knot at the back of her head. "If those bitches hurt you, I promise I'm about to go hurt them."

"Damn straight," I echoed, trying to reassure the kid. Poppy's fear hadn't dialed down one iota.

Darby crossed the room, perching on the edge of the couch by Poppy's feet. The blanket she'd been covered with was my favorite, the cloud-like fabric both soft and lightweight. Poppy ran her tiny fingers over it in what seemed like a nervous tick.

"Can you tell me what happened?" Darby cooed softly, and I would have given anything to have had her around when I was new to this world. Cold and alone and scared out of my mind, how much better would it have been with someone—hell, anyone—to give a shit about me when I was scared?

After a bout of a trembling lip, Poppy opened her mouth to answer, only to snap it shut again when a ruckus sounded from upstairs. Stomping feet echoed throughout the room as Harper and Sarina—well, more Sarina than Harper—raced down the staircase.

"Wait for us!" Sarina cried as a disgruntled Harper trailed behind her.

"Oracle," Sarina grumbled, answering a question no one asked aloud. "How many times do I have to say this?" Sarina plopped down on the adjacent love seat, yanking Harper down with her. "Okay, go."

"Stop policing my thoughts, weirdo," Darby chided, and Poppy's eyes grew wide. Darby shot a disgruntled look at Sarina before reassuring the kid. "Don't worry about Sarina. She's a sweetheart, promise."

The agent rolled her eyes as she practically bounced in her seat. "Tell her, kiddo. She'll be pissed, but she's on your side."

Poppy drew back as Harper elbowed Sarina in the ribs. "Quit freaking out the small child, dude. Some oracle you are."

I stared at the ceiling, trying not to start yelling at the pair and their antics. Some psychics they were.

"It's a madhouse in here, kid," Darby muttered. "You get used to it. Can you tell me what happened to you?"

Poppy's tiny fingers reached for Darby's hand, and she freely gave it to her. "I don't know where to start. I don't know..." She trailed off, shrugging. "So much of it doesn't make sense. For weeks people have been acting strange. Not behaving like they used to, not doing their normal things, and when I touch the places they have, it doesn't feel like them."

I sat up straighter. I'd heard of something like that before. These kinds of psychics were called something special. I'd come across a few black-market rings trying to procure psychic slaves to spy on their enemies. They'd been looking primarily for children, wanting to get them young before they could remember their parents. Well, they *had* been before I dismantled their entire enterprise at the business end of my fangs.

"I'm sorry, I don't think I understand. What do you mean?"

Poppy rolled her eyes and shook her head. "Sorry. I —I'm a kind of a…"

"In the arcane world, we call you a diviner. It's psychometry," Sarina murmured, likely reading the pictures in Poppy's head. "The word you're looking for. You touch objects and get an impression or a vision off of them, right?"

"Yeah, that's what Shiloh called it. A diviner." Poppy's gaze dropped to her fingers again. "She's in trouble. I tried to get her out, but with her leg, I couldn't get her to the window."

Darby sat forward on the cushion. "Who is in trouble? Where did you come from?"

Poppy's breath hitched. "Shiloh. She and I were locked in the basement—have been for what feels like a week. I was asking too many questions, and this woman locked me up. I'd never seen her before, but she… hit me, hurt me. When Shiloh saved me, I thought I wouldn't have to go through that again, but there I was —only this time was worse. These people were supposed to be my home—they were supposed to keep me safe."

Tears tracked down Poppy's face, but she wiped them off just as fast as they fell. "I need to save Shiloh. The rest of them can all die for all I care, but she saved me. Put herself in the way of that woman."

"Son of a bitch," Sarina hissed, her eyes getting a far-off quality that put me on edge.

"Let me guess—my mother?" Darby growled, her whole body vibrating as her fingers got a flickering glow to them that I'd quickly learned was a sign she was about to lose it.

Sarina stared at the kid, giving her a nod. "The ring, the one you lifted off of her. Give it to Darby."

The child frowned, her left hand pulling back as if she was trying to hide whatever was in her fist.

Sarina raised her eyebrow at the girl, the no-nonsense pull of it making me sit back in my seat. "She'll keep it safe. Promise."

Poppy's gaze flitted from Sarina to Harper, then to me before landing on Darby. "You have to keep it from the man. It's not meant for him. He'll steal it and make it wrong. You have to keep it safe. If you don't..." She trailed off, shaking her head. "You'll see when you touch it. It's not meant for him, and he shouldn't have it."

"Meant for who?" Darby whispered, but she hadn't needed to ask. We both knew the answer to that question.

Poppy held out her fist, and Darby opened her hand under it. Then the kid dropped a heavy silver ring in my sister's palm, a large black stone practically shimmering in the low light. The thick band had familiar sigils carved into the metal. Sigils that I'd only seen in one place—engraved in the door that led out of the In-Between.

My gut tightened as a familiar buzz overtook my whole body. What the hell was this kid doing with Azrael's ring? And it had to be his, had to be.

"None of this makes any sense," Darby muttered, echoing my thoughts exactly.

"Of course it does," Hildy said, making both Darby and I about jump out of our skins. He'd been MIA while the boys had gone to destroy the training room, so his sudden appearance shocked the hell out of the two of us who could see him. "My daughter's used and abused her power and authority as she's always done. She's infiltrated a covens' home, used them and their power for her own gain. She's gone against everythin' I taught her. Everything." Pain etched lines in his face as a silvery tear trailed down his cheek.

But the "why's" were still a mystery. Why would this

woman side with our brother? Why would she go against her own daughter? Why—

Darby gasped as Poppy closed her palm over the ring, latching onto her hand with a white-knuckled grip.

Then the shit really hit the fan.

5

Darby's entire body went rigid as her breath hitched and then stopped altogether. Her eyes were open, but she stared straight through Poppy as if she wasn't there anymore. Before I knew it, I was off my feet, ready to tear Darby away from the child holding her captive.

"Don't," Sarina barked, latching onto my wrist before I could rip my sister away. "She has to see it for herself. She has to know the truth."

Flinging Sarina's hand off me, I barely managed to hold myself back from baring my fangs. "The truth according to who?"

Sarina shook her head at me like I was a simpering child. "Who do you think? You know whose ring that is. I saw it on your face the second you recognized those sigils. Poppy is letting her see the ring's history—information Darby needs if she's to do what she has to."

I'd always thought Sarina was a lovely woman, but right then, I was having trouble not decking the agent. "So, Azrael set this all up, then? What are you, his minion?"

She shook her head again, clucking her tongue at me. "You know better than that, Sloane. You know damn well what it is to be one of us. How is what I see any different from what you see when you read someone's blood? I have no control over the messages I'm given, no more than you do when you taste the flavor of a damned soul. I can't read your mind or future, but I know enough to know that the path you have in front of you is not the same as your sister's."

It might have been childish, but I rolled my eyes and reached for Darby again, the scent of fear and rage and desperation high on the air. Sarina's fingers tightened on my wrist again before I peeled them off, practically grinding my teeth so I didn't crush her delicate bones in my hand. "ABI agent or not, you touch me again, and we're going to have problems."

"You can't touch her. What is meant for her is not meant for you," Sarina insisted, placing herself in between us. "You can flash your fangs and growl all you want, but I'm doing this for you, too. She has to be the one to accept this knowledge. It's her burden to bear, not yours."

I was sorely tempted to bodily move her out of my way or punt her into the surface of the sun—I couldn't decide which—when I felt the whole room go wired. A wall of rage rankled on the air long before the soft shuffle of footsteps whispered down the stairs.

Bastian and Thomas were in this room, their scents reaching me before their steps did, but it was Bishop's unmitigated fury that felt like an actual physical thing.

"What the fuck, Sarina?" Bishop growled from behind me, damn near knocking me out of the way to get to Darby. He reached for her shoulders, yanking her out of Poppy's grip, and that was the exact second I smelled the blood. He cradled my sister in his arms, her skin damn near blue as bloody teardrops fell from her eyes.

My bottom lip started to tremble as I watched Darby continue to wilt, the red of the bloody teardrops so stark on her skin.

Why isn't she breathing? Why is she crying blood? What the fuck is going on?

"Azrael, you get your feathery ass here right now," I yelled, my head tilted back as I shouted at the ceiling. But not only did he not show himself, that cold pit of dread had returned. He wasn't going to come and help.

"We're too warded," Bastian muttered. "He can't hear you, love."

Tears pooled in my eyes as I rounded on the man I loved. "Then summon him or yank him here or drop the war—" I blinked for a second before I raced out the glass French doors that led to the backyard. The weight of the ward was a physical thing, and I knew the instant I crossed it. "Azrael, please. Please ju—"

The air shimmered right in front of me like waves of heat coming up from hot asphalt after a summer rain as my stomach dropped to my toes. Then my father appeared out of thin air. Dark hair, pale skin, black feathers, coal-black suit—the standard fare for the Angel of Death, minus the scythe.

Violet eyes assessed me for a moment, irritation pinching his face. "My ass is not feathery," he scolded, his eyebrow hitched up in parental affront.

I blinked at him for a second, realizing all too quickly that he'd heard me when I'd called for him. He'd heard and ignored me, the dick. "That is not the point, and you know it. Darby needs your help."

His wings shivered a bit before winking out of sight. "No, she doesn't."

"I don't know about you, but not breathing and crying blood sounds like a whole-ass ailment to me.

Wanna lend a hand?" Azrael's face hardened, his hair flickering from white to black and back again.

Jesus, fuck. When will I learn to shut my mouth?

Azrael huffed, his gaze moving from me to something over my shoulder. I followed his gaze to see Bastian frantically searching the lawn for me as if I weren't standing right in front of him. "He can't see us. We're not on his plane." I needed a second to digest that little tidbit, but Azrael didn't give it to me. "Your sister is far more resilient than you give her credit for, and she doesn't need my help. Listen to the oracle, will you?"

I was still stuck on the us being "not on his plane" bullshit, but Darby didn't have the time or oxygen for me to ask. "I'd love to listen to her if she were telling me anything, but she isn't. And I have a feeling you know why."

He rolled his eyes, turning away from me as he surveyed the tall grass. "You'll know when the time is right. Now, quit hounding me. She'll wake up soon enough."

Well, this had been a *complete* waste of my time. Now I just needed to figure out how in the hell to get back home.

Azrael shifted back just a little, his wings making another appearance as he prepared to leave. "A storm is coming, kid. And I didn't get to teach you everything I needed to. Just remember, when she asks you for a favor? Tell her yes."

I opened my mouth to yell at him for giving me such stupid, vague-as-fuck advice when my stomach dropped again. The air shimmered all around me as Azrael disappeared—or rather, as I reappeared. One second, I was about to give my stupid father a piece of my mind, and the next, I was engulfed in Bastian's arms and lifted off my feet.

"Don't do that to me again. You hear me?" he growled into my hair, his hold on me so tight it was almost painful. But under that strength was a trembling sort of fear that I knew all too well. I could practically taste his bitter relief on my tongue. "I thought I'd lost you. Thought I'd be like that miserable bloke in our living room."

I wanted to explain, but we didn't have the time. Darby was going to wake up any minute, and I needed to be there when she did. "We need to go. She'll be coming around soon."

He gave me a startled huff as I slipped from his grasp and latched onto his wrist, dragging him behind me as I marched right back to the house. Azrael hadn't given me anything I could use, nor had he provided even a shred of a goddamn clue as to what I was supposed to be doing. Other than a cryptic "grant her a favor" bullshit, I was at a loss.

"Breathe, baby. I need you to breathe," Bishop pleaded, brushing the blood from Darby's cheeks as he rocked her in his lap.

As if he'd commanded it from the heavens, Darby sucked in a gasping breath. The color started to return to her skin, as more blood fell from her closed lids into her blonde hair, staining it scarlet.

"There you go, baby. Just keep breathing." Bishop's breath hitched as tears ran down his face.

Darby's eyelids fluttered, and for the first time since I saw her in his arms, her skin damn near blue from lack of oxygen, did I take a breath of my own.

"Wh-what happened?" she croaked, the shattered glass of a voice making my stomach drop.

Bishop bent and kissed her forehead, his jaw tightening like he was two steps away from losing it. "You stopped breathing. Your heart stopped beating. You started crying blood. And then Sarina couldn't hear you anymore. She couldn't see inside your mind. We thought... We tried calling Azrael, but he wouldn't come. God, baby, I thought we'd lost you."

She flinched like he'd slapped her, and I watched a haunted sort of knowledge come over her before she staggered to her feet, ignoring all of us when we insisted she sit back down.

"I need a phone. Now," she ordered, holding out a hand for one, like it was no big deal that she hadn't been breathing a minute ago—like she should be standing at all.

Simon, of all people, slapped his slim Night Watch issued phone in her hand, and without so much as a peep, Darby dialed a number from memory. I practically felt the rings all the way across the room, their trills rattling in my chest as I watched her put the phone up to her ear. When a childlike voice answered, I knew whatever was coming was going to be bad.

"This better be who I think it is, or you're going to have hell to pay," the person on the other end of the line griped, and as much as I wanted to smile, I couldn't. Ingrid Dubois might have sounded like a kid, but the ancient vampire had to be a thousand if she was a day. And I never wanted to find out what kind of hell she could dish out.

"Ing," Darby wheezed, "I need to call in my favor."

When she asks you for a favor, tell her yes.

But Darby didn't ask me for a favor. She'd asked Ingrid. Still...

"About damn time. Jesus. You've held onto the fucking thing for five years. Is this just my favor or the whole nest, because I gotta say, sweetheart, this week has been a fucking doozy."

Well, she's not wrong.

Darby seemed to think about it for about half a millisecond. "The whole nest, both boons from Mags, *and* the *three* favors you owe me. And even then, I might have to take out a marker."

The silence on the other end of the line was deafening, and the weight of it in this room was a physical thing pressing down on my shoulders. "I will say one thing about you, Adler. You sure as shit are a go big or go home kind of girl."

"It's bad, Ing," Darby croaked. "Worse than the attack on the nest."

Bastian clutched my hand tighter in his. Thomas had filled us in on the attack on the Dubois nest. It wasn't just *bad*. It had damn near been a catastrophe. Several mid-level members of the nest had been killed, and Ingrid herself barely made it out intact.

"And this is coming for us all?" Ingrid asked, and Darby looked up at Bishop, her eyes pleading before shifting her gaze to me. She didn't need to ask for any sort of favor for me to back her up. Not with her blue eyes blazing like the Devil himself was knocking on her door.

"If I can stop it, no. If I can't…" Darby trailed off,

but I knew. That look on her face told of devastation and death and the end of all good things.

"Consider it done. Thomas will tell you where we are. Meet in three hours, yes?"

She nodded, even though Ingrid couldn't see her, but I could, and there was a bitter defeat in that single head bob.

"Three hours," she agreed and pressed the red "END CALL" button.

Bishop cupped her cheeks as my gut bottomed out. "Tell me. What is it?"

"It's war."

6

W ar had me watching my sister make one decision after another with no real choices in the matter. It had me standing idly by while she had to choose between her own life—her own safety—and the fate of us all. It had me biting my tongue and trying not to make this whole mess worse for her. It also had me eye to eye with the dirt as we hid in the trees and waited for "the signal."

What that signal might be could be anything from a massive explosion or a hole ripped in the fabric of space. Really, it was a toss-up.

I'd never been to Haunted Peak before, and while it wasn't much bigger than the town I'd grown up in, it did have a few things mine didn't. A giant mountain prison with a lake on top, if it being the main one. The only thing keeping me sane was Bastian's heat at my right and the knowledge that I was free to mow down anyone standing in my way.

"You all right, love?" Bastian murmured, and I shot him an incredulous glare. He knew full well we were way too close to a local ghoul nest who had just as good of hearing as I did to be asking that question.

The same damn ghoul nest that had kidnapped Darby's adoptive father and best friend, J. The same one that was in league with her mother.

The same one that would pounce on us in a hot second if they caught wind that we were here.

Also, being downwind from this vile ghoul nest smelled like malice and dirty socks.

Truth be told, I was not a fan of the current plan. I wasn't too keen on Darby trying to pull the wool over her mother's eyes, no more than I was in favor of her trying to burn herself up just so her mom didn't latch onto a boatload of power. I'd just gotten a glimpse of this woman in my life, and now... Now she might...

Was I all right? No, the fuck I wasn't.

But I didn't get a say—not about this.

Because there wasn't a better plan or another way out. Even if I wanted to take her place—and I really did—I wasn't capable of doing what Darby could. And I couldn't take this away from her, either. Because if it were my family up on the chopping block, I'd be doing the same fucking thing she was. If it were my dad, if it were my best friend, if it were my people, I'd be in her shoes in a heartbeat.

And that just sucked.

My face must have shown the despair, the utter uselessness I felt, because he pressed his shoulder more into me—the best he could do since hugging was off the table. His green eyes warmed in sympathy, and it was all I could do to not start bawling. Over the last three hours I had argued and pleaded and did my best to think of something—anything—else but what we were doing.

A faint rustling to our left pulled my gaze from Bastian to a very small, very ancient vampire. Ingrid was up a tree playing lookout, while the rest of us strategically positioned ourselves in a choke ring just outside the target area. She was also sticking her tongue out at me. If I didn't know better, I'd have thought she was finally regressing to the age she had been when she was turned. But since I was the youngest of us, I pulled the same face, adding an almost silent raspberry for good measure before I faced forward again.

It was the waiting that was killing me. Right then my sister was pretending her way through a pretty dicey situation as she tried to fake out a master manipulator, and here I was just sitting on my ass staring at dirt.

Then I heard an ear-piercing whistle followed quickly by a chorus of bellows and screams. It seemed like that was our cue. Bastian and I popped up from the ground together, weapons drawn and raced toward the ghouls and witches in league with Darby's certified bitch of a mother. Only... only it seemed like the two were fighting each other rather than waiting for us. Witches shot blistering spells at the ghouls as a few of the giant arcaners ripped into the woman with their blunted teeth.

I skidded to a stop as I watched a Knoxville witch wrench her glowing hands apart, the spell working its magic to rip the head clean off a ghoul's neck. Shooting a glance over my shoulder I met Bastian's eyes. He shrugged, lifting his chin at the occupied witches and drew a thumb across his neck.

He didn't have to tell me twice.

Stowing the sword in its sheath, I raced for the witch and latched onto her neck like it was a Capri Sun. Two pulls in and I wanted to wretch at the vileness of her blood, so I yanked out my fangs and snapped her neck for good measure. Darby had said there was a chance that these witches had been conned or spelled, but this one sure hadn't, and the horrors in her blood were deserving of a death sentence no matter who was meting it out.

Spitting the blood on the forest floor, I moved to the next person in my way, uncertain if I would kill them or just knock them out. My internal debate was quickly settled, as a ghoul rushed me with the swiftness of a jungle cat, coupled with the bearing of a linebacker. With a smile on my face, I sliced through his throat without so much as a hiccup, his body beginning to dissolve before his head even hit the ground. I caught sight of Bastian mowing down ghoul and witch alike, taking heads with zero compunction just like I was. But there were so many, the nest larger than I'd thought, and with so many witches in the mix, I quickly lost him in the melee.

I didn't like that I couldn't see Bastian, or that I was so far from my sister, and I absolutely hated that I couldn't wrap up all my friends in fucking bubble wrap and stick them in my pocket so they couldn't get hurt. Honestly? All I wanted was to get to point A—AKA, here—to point B—wherever the fuck Darby was—with no issues and zero injuries. A want that was dashed thirty seconds later when a fireball zipped through the air toward me, while I was busy cutting off a ghoul's head.

I saw the thing about two seconds too late and had

to duck to avoid it before the ghoul was properly dispatched. While it was semi-satisfying to see the ball of flames explode against the ghoul's chest, it was significantly less so, once I found myself the target of this witch's next missile. The ghoul bellowed his rage and pain at being set ablaze as I tried to use him as a flailing—albeit on fire—shield.

The results weren't entirely successful.

Sparks exploded against the ghoul's back, the embers catching my right arm and the side of my face in a sear of what should have been white-hot agony that I barely felt. Unerringly, my gaze found the offending witch, a tiny redheaded thing with freckles for fuck's sake. If it weren't for the shit-eating grin that spread across her face, I might have thought she was innocent, but the absolute glee pissed me all the way off. She launched her next attack, another ball of bullshit fire forming in her palm, but I was ready this time. With a swift swing of my blade, I dispatched the ghoul in my way before showing this girl just how fast I could be when I was pissed off. Before she could launch the orb at me, my blade was at her throat.

It was funny, but a few months ago, I would have bit first and asked questions later. But after tasting Bastian's blood, after realizing what evil really tasted like, I couldn't make myself bite the woman. Especially after tasting her coven member only moments before. I didn't want that vile stink in my throat, and I didn't want to know what horrors were hiding beneath her flesh.

Killing her would just have to do. A single flick of my blade and the witch was dead, her body falling in a heap at my feet.

I was almost to the lakeshore just past the tree line when I heard Darby's scream, the sound of heart-rending agony meeting my ears like an echo of my own loss. I knew that sound, knew it so well, I might as well have screamed it myself. Darby was losing someone she loved, and there wasn't a damn thing I could do about it.

But maybe…

My feet flew of their own accord, racing toward that dreadful sound, while my brain tried and failed to catch up to the picture in front of me. Two men were tied to thick wooden stakes buried in the sand: a tall blond man and a slightly shorter dark-haired one. Both had been beaten, the scent of their fear and blood and pain rent high on the air.

But Darby was clutching the blond man to her as his legs gave out and she sank with him to the sand. She screamed and cried but her pleas for help went unanswered, and I knew hope was all but gone when Azrael glided over the sand. For a fleeting second, I thought he might help the man in her arms, but the sadness on his face told the tale without a single spoken word.

In that instant, my heart broke because I knew that resignation, that defeat. I'd seen it on my mother's face when she had known she wouldn't be able to save me, and it was that same damn expression lurking on Azrael's then. It was a helplessness that I, too, felt and had no idea how to remedy.

With a flick of his wrist, Azrael beckoned a fluttering light from the blond man in Darby's arms. The light flickered over the sand, too, as if pulled by a string as Azrael held his arms wide. In a matter of moments, the light speared into his chest, fading out of sight before Darby ever knew he was there. Another scream bubbled up Darby's throat, this one louder and more devastating than the last. The earth rumbled beneath our feet, nearly knocking me to the ground as Darby's pain made itself known.

She pressed a shaky kiss to the man's forehead and stood, and it didn't matter that this man was an unknown to me. It didn't matter that I didn't know if he was her father or her friend. None of it mattered because my sister was dying inside, and I couldn't do a damn thing to help.

A tall woman shrouded in darkness struggled

against the hold of a giant Viking-looking Fae. The shadows surrounding the woman moved like ink in water, almost oily as they played Peek-a-boo to the soul underneath. That darkness made my stomach turn, and I didn't have to taste the woman's blood to know who she was.

Darby made a beeline for her mother, an orb of pure light forming in my sister's palm as she assessed the woman dispassionately. Without so much as a blip of emotion on her face, she shoved that orb down her mother's throat and patiently waited while Mariana burned up from the inside out.

It was justice, sure, but it made my skin crawl. My feet decided to start moving again, the bitter detachment on Darby's face a little too close to what I'd done a year ago. She couldn't do what I did—she couldn't fall down that bitter path of revenge and wrath. It would burn her up in the end.

Darby had too much to lose—too much to leave behind. I hadn't, and I didn't want her to torch her whole life. I'd just picked up speed when it seemed like the whole world stopped—the air in my lungs, the birds in the sky, the sounds of the still-going battle. Ghouls mid-strike and witches mid-spell froze, their magic and weapons halting midair. My entire body locked for a moment, my limbs refusing to heed my commands, but something told me to keep going, to keep pushing.

Quicksand had nothing on this. Hell, it was like running in wet cement.

My first thought was that this had to be Darby. Somehow, some way, my sister had stopped the world, stopped time, stopped everything, and half of me couldn't blame her. Oh, how I had wished for it all to stop when I'd realized that my parents were dead. When I understood that it wasn't a lie, and no one was coming back.

When I knew I was alone.

My heart ached in my chest, the echo of grief making it hard to swallow as I pushed forward. Only my next step fell as if there was nothing holding me back, the return of my speed frightening me more than anything else. I raced past the sprawling mansions on the shore and into the trees where my sister held her hands aloft, a group of ghouls caught in the web of the too-potent power thrumming in her veins. A quick flick of her wrists and the ghoul's head popped off, thumping to the ground in a wet sort of splat.

While convenient, the ease at which Darby killed them had bile racing up my throat. Hypocritical, I know. What? Was I the only one allowed to kill without an ounce of remorse? Was I the only one who could take vengeance for wrongs done to me?

While the answer was "No," it was also not a resounding "Yes." Sloane Cabot was dead. Darby Adler was not.

Hildy tried reasoning with her, but what good was a ghost in the face of such pain?

"I know your minds. Your names. Your sins," she murmured, but her voice wasn't just on the air, it was in my head, too. I got a sinking feeling she'd done that on purpose. "Your betrayal has been noted. You are not welcome here. Twenty-four hours. Get the *fuck* out of my town. Get your shit out of Knoxville. Out of my state. If I see you, there is no place in this world or the next safe for you."

"Are you sure you want to be doing this, lass?" Hildy pleaded, stark fear on his ghostly face, but Darby didn't see it. She wouldn't even look at him.

What she did do was shrug, still staring in the distance as witches and ghouls heeded her warning and fled. "Your daughter set this into motion ages ago—all I'm doing is making me and mine safe."

Hildy got right in her face, begging Darby to listen to him. "You're painting a target on your back is what you're doing. Disbanding covens and nests? You realize you're taking the mantle of leader if you do that. Have you thought this through?"

Determination fell over her features, solidifying them into a mask of wrath. "If you think I'm going to let this stand, you're out of your mind. Twenty-four hours is a goddamn gift, and you know it."

She'd given those that betrayed her a day to get out of town.

Was it a gift?

Probably.

Would it bite her in the ass?

Absolutely.

Was I going to be there to back her up?

Without question.

She just had to let me.

7

Funerals were for the birds.

No, that wasn't quite right. While funerals in general were indeed the absolute worst, *Southern* funerals were a level of torture reserved for the deepest pits of Hell. It wasn't just the endless casseroles and impromptu visitors. It was the near-constant gawking and grief-glutting that made me sick to my stomach. Was this what I would have had to deal with if I hadn't died that night along with my parents? A slew of rubberneckers practically doom-scrolling through my life? Given the state of distress lurking in Darby's eyes, I was sort of happy I was left with the direct-to-grave approach.

Over the last few days, I had been keeping an eye out for Darby, helping her arrange her father's funeral, but more than that, I was watching her back and making sure she didn't fly off the handle. She had painted a pretty big target on her back up at the lake, sure, but I was more worried about the thing she *wasn't* talking about—namely the mass of souls she'd absorbed emptying Azrael's ring, executing her mother, and watching her father pass away before her very eyes.

Every so often, in the height of Darby's stress, the house would rattle, or wind would whip inside, or all the power would go out, and we'd have to do damage control. Either Darby's best friend, J, Bishop, or I would usher whatever visitor that had dropped by—totally unannounced—out before they realized that it wasn't nature causing the ruckus. After less than a day, we figured out that keeping visitors out altogether was the best idea.

Darby's skin was a permanent shade of ashen, with twin dark circles under her eyes that resisted the efforts of even the strongest concealer. She tried to sleep—or at least she said she did—but I still heard her rustling in her bed, tossing and turning or screaming herself awake in the middle of the night.

The day of the funeral, the whole of us were acting like skittish cats, waiting for the next shoe to drop, the sense that something was coming high on the air. Or maybe that was just me.

"You ready to go?" I croaked, offering my sister a tall blue mug filled with the strongest coffee I'd ever smelled. I, too, was sipping from my own mug, the daylight hour playing havoc with my sleep schedule. Fidgeting, I pulled at the collar of my blouse as I waited for her to answer.

Instead, she downed half the mug of scalding coffee in one gulp before setting it down to stir in a spoonful of sugar. Her mouth twitched like she was remembering something, and a lone tear streaked down her cheek. Silently, she dashed the wetness away, lifted her mug, and drained the rest of it.

"Not really," she murmured, her voice thick. "I don't think I'll ever be ready."

Yep, definitely preferred the direct-to-grave route. Anything was better than parading my grief around in front of the entire town. Why did people do this? Was it a torture kink or something? The whole thing sounded awful. A service followed by a graveside gathering and then coffee and cake after? It all sounded like a complete nightmare.

We managed to make it through the service without too many issues. Personally, if Darby hadn't insisted on the whole thing, I would have tried to hide her under a rock until she got herself together. Inexplicably, she managed to hold her shit together with only a minor light flickering issue at the church and a small gale at the graveside gathering. Both could be explained away, but I knew it was only a matter of time before she eventually lost her shit.

Bastian was a warm presence at my side as I kept an eye out for my sister. Somehow, he knew just how horrible this was—not just for her, but for me, too. It had only been a year since my family died, only a year since they had been ripped from me, and here I was trying to be strong for a sister I barely knew in a weird little town with far too many arcaners to count.

The wind picked up a bit more as the preacher droned on and on at the graveside, Darby's composure slipping just a little bit more with every extraneous word. Without thought, my feet propelled me to her, and I rested my head on her shoulder for comfort. "Nothing I say can ever make this better. It fucking sucks. And it'll suck for a while." This I knew for a damn fact. "But, you're my big sister, and you know…" I paused, squeezing her withering frame in a sideways hug. "Well, we've got each other. You've always got me

to shout at, tell me to go fuck myself, cry, you know…
the things big sisters do."

She leaned her head against mine. "I'll remember
that. I'm glad we have each other. Glad I found you."
But her voice got thick, and she didn't say another
word.

With a nod, I squeezed her shoulder and went back
to Bastian, allowing his heat and touch to ease my pain.
When it came time to toss dirt on her father's grave,
Darby lost what little hold she had on her grief, the
ground shaking in her wake as she marched away from
the crowd to gather herself. I watched her go, keeping
half an ear on the preacher and most of my attention
on her.

She picked a bench to sit on, and I slipped through
the crowd as soon as it was polite to do so. I didn't want
to blow Darby's cover here—being a police officer and
all—but I had the distinct feeling that there were far
more arcaners in this town than she knew about. A
varied few batted an eye when the ground pitched, the
majority taking it in stride as if earthquakes were an
everyday occurrence and random wind gusts were no
big deal. Hell, there wasn't even a stir when the lights in
the church went out, or the candles in the sanctuary
flared to life of their own accord for a moment before
snuffing out altogether.

As soon as I was free of the crowd, I made a beeline for Darby, her fists propping up her chin as tears fell down her cheeks. A man approached her, his crisp gray suit and white hair turning my stomach before I even caught sight of his face. I knew that suit, that hair, that swagger. I'd seen it a year ago as he sauntered over to murder my mother, his steps just as fluid and unhurried as they had been on the day my parents died.

Before I could yell out her name, she stood, facing off against our brother without so much as a nod to her own safety. Her gaze roamed the cemetery, skirting over me as if she hadn't realized I was there before returning to Essex. Her words were muffled, and she turned away, giving him her back. My feet propelled me faster. She had no idea just how dangerous he was—no idea just how quickly he could strike.

But I did.

As someone who had been killed—technically twice —by this man already, I wasted no time on propriety or social norms. I hauled ass across the graveyard like my life—or rather her life—depended on it.

But by the time I got to her side, Essex was gone, the bastard floating away on a fucking breeze or some shit, and all that was left behind was another freaking note. Propped jauntily in the grass, his lazy scrawl made me rage as I read the words.

Azrael lied to you. Killian isn't where you think he is.

Come find me when you're ready for the truth.

—Essex

The truth? What would he know about the truth?

Darby took one look at that note, and her eye twitched as she ground her teeth before she turned away. I couldn't blame her. I was tempted to scent him out, aching to track him down like the dog he was and... The ground pitched beneath my feet, and it seemed for the first time, Darby actually noticed.

Over the last few days, she'd seemed entirely unaware that she'd been wreaking havoc, but now—when it was all too impossible to contain—she realized the issue. Or it was because both of us got knocked on our asses. That could be it, too.

With my butt on the grass and my rage nearly exploding out of my ears, I peered at the too-fancy cardstock and my brother's bullshit scrawl. I didn't believe a single word on that paper. Whatever this was, it had to be a trap of some kind. Essex was fucking famous for those. How many people had he killed, how much death had been met out by his hands? I didn't trust Azrael as far as I could throw him, but Essex? I'd rather cut off my own arm and solder it to my forehead than believe a single word he had to say.

Darby reached for the cardstock, but I smacked her hand away before her fingers could make contact. The last time I'd touched one of Essex's notes, I'd turned into a flickering *Skeletor* party decoration. That fate was not going to befall my sister. No way, no how. Plus, anything that came from him was highly suspect and sure to be filled with booby-traps.

"Are you okay?" Stupidly, that was the first thing that came out of my mouth, the annoying epithet making Darby grind her teeth—she was likely so tired of hearing it.

She rolled her eyes, rubbing the hand I'd smacked, seeming to come back to herself. "Of course I'm not okay. Are you okay?"

Was I?

No, I could honestly say that I was not. And why would I be? The man that murdered my parents just strolled through this cemetery without a care in the world. He just fucking walked in here. There weren't any sirens or a disturbance in the force. Nothing held him back, and no one kicked him out. And nothing was stopping him from doing it again. There was nothing to keep him out or prevent him from walking right up to us and slitting our throats next.

"No," I croaked. "No, I'm not okay."

Warm hands closed around the top of my shoulders, pulling me to my feet. Bastian's bottle-green gaze bore into me, but all I felt was my too-hot skin prickle as my jaw clenched so hard, I thought I was going to break my teeth. His fingers threaded through my hair, and he pressed my face into his shoulder.

"Your face, love," he whispered when I resisted, and it dawned on me that Darby wasn't the only person losing it today. "Breathe, Sloane. Tell me what happened."

Darby let out a snort. "Our bastard of a brother is what happened. See for yourself."

But Bastian didn't look. Instead, he pulled back, cupping my face in his hands as he looked me over. "I will in a moment," he murmured.

How do I protect her? How do I keep her safe? And will she even let me?

Bastian's mouth didn't move at all, but I heard his voice in my head all the same. It was what settled the storm in me, the turbulent waves crashing in my head quieting just a little so I could think.

"I'm okay. We're all okay," I lied, sucking in deep

breaths, so I didn't just fucking lose it all over this overly crowded cemetery.

Bastian's mouth twisted, but he let me get away with my bald-faced lie, breaking his gaze away to stare at the cardstock in the grass. His grip on me only got tighter as his jaw clenched, the truth of the situation coming to light far faster than I thought it would. My grip on him got tighter as well, and rather than plan and strategize or comfort Darby or get us the hell out of there, I dropped my forehead, resting it against his chest. The welcome beat of his heart echoed through my whole body, and I breathed in his scent.

He was here and alive. I was here with him—not so much alive, but close enough. The world was still turning, my sister was still breathing. We were okay, right?

Right?

Pulling my face out of Bastian's chest, I met his gaze, and a flicker of a smile spread across his lips. "Back to normal already. I suppose this is unnecessary then."

He reached into his pocket and pulled out a necklace with a familiar purple stone. It wasn't the same glamoured necklace that had been burned off me a few days ago, but it was a close enough replica that I had to do a double take. I took the chain from his fingers, fastening it around my neck as fast as I could. I had a feeling I'd be needing it soon enough.

I felt more than heard Thomas and Bishop approach, with Darby's best friend J and his boyfriend Jimmy trailing closely behind.

Thomas took one look at the note on the ground and rolled his eyes. "You know that's a trap, right?"

I narrowed my eyes at him. "No shit."

8

The evidence bag plastic did nothing to hide the note's intended purpose. I stared at it as it rested on Darby's coffee table, the offending paper tucked safely inside so it couldn't poison us or kill us or whatever it was intended to do. Crammed on the couch, I sat half on top of Bastian, while Thomas' shoulder pressed into mine, and Simon perched awkwardly with Dahlia on his lap. Five people weren't meant for this piece of furniture, but since all the other chairs and most of the floor was occupied, I kept my trap shut. After Essex's appearance at the cemetery, most of us decided to skip the reception at Darby's father's house in favor of a strategy session at hers.

Too bad there had been zero strategy and a hell of a lot of silence.

Darby and Bishop sat in a cerulean velvet armchair with gold nail head trim and a jaunty winged back, her legs rested on the armrest, and Bishop had her head tucked under his chin. Her eyes were closed, and one would think she was sleeping if it weren't for the little tremors rattling the house every so often. Well, that and about every sixty seconds or so she would clench her fists so hard her knuckles turned white, and the lamps would buzz and flicker like they were about to explode.

She wanted out of this house. She wanted to be out on the street searching for the witches who betrayed her, or maybe she wanted to take some ghoul heads. Hell, I was pretty sure she'd be happy with just going back to work, but that wasn't an option, either. No, her options were hamstringed by the souls rattling around in her body and our asshole brother lurking in the shadows somewhere.

What am I supposed to do, Azrael? I mentally pleaded for him to hear me. *So, yeah, those souls didn't kill her right away or anything, but this isn't good. No one save for a deity is supposed to have that much power.*

But as was his norm, Azrael not only refused to show his face, but he also didn't illuminate any answers, either. Of course, I had an idea of what could be done, but I didn't think anyone was going to like it.

I sure as hell didn't.

"So, no one is going to say anything about the penchant for earthquakes this house has?" Harper griped from the floor, her head resting on Sarina's lap. "Or the fact that this one is so juiced up she might as well power a nuclear reactor?" She hooked her thumb at Darby as she stared at the ceiling. "I mean, I'm all for trying to gather oneself and hiding away, but holy shit, girl, you light up like Vegas every twelve minutes, and a single temper tantrum from you is going to break the planet."

Eyes still closed, Darby snorted. "Tell me how you really feel, Harper. Don't hold back."

"That *was* me sugarcoating it, sweetheart. You don't want to hear everything I have to say."

As someone who had been on the other end of a Harper tongue-lashing, I winced. Darby opened a lone eye, spearing Harper with an irritated half-glare.

"Maybe I do." Darby opened the other eye and sat up. "Maybe I want to know what you're holding back."

Oh, this has disaster written all over it.

Harper mirrored her, rising from her Sarina pillow to stare Darby down. "You have too much power running through your veins, no outlet, and you're shaking the fucking planet. Not to mention, no one has said a peep about whether or not the souls roiling under your skin are being put to rest, or what's going to happen now that you've essentially blew up two Knoxville factions. Your father died and that is awful. Truly, I feel for you, but you have too much going on to just sit here and wallow, especially when you're waving a red fucking flag in front of your brother."

Harper stood, and I was too stunned that all my fears were just spewing out of her mouth to do anything else but just sit there.

"I feel them whispering under your skin, and I know you do, too. Those souls aren't at rest, and they aren't at peace. You're just another prison for them, and Essex Drake just walked up to you like you were a cute little toddler. I have to wonder why he's not terrified of you, and when I think about that too hard, I get scared."

Exactly zero things about what Harper said were wrong, and Darby seemed to know it, too, because she stared at my small friend and simply nodded. "I'm scared, too. But I don't know if I can fix it or even how I'm supposed to. Azrael is MIA again, and... I don't trust myself to go up against Essex. I don't trust myself to walk out in public or say hi to my neighbors or go back to work. I'm just trying to breathe here."

Squeezing Bastian's hand, I offered the solution I'd been mentally deliberating for about forty-eight hours. "Why can't we put the souls back in the ring? Your body can't hold them without causing seismic activity, right? And you're not absorbing them like normal. Then, why can't we just shove them back in the ring, pawn it off to Azrael, and have his feathery ass deal with it?"

I had a feeling things wouldn't go that smoothly, but it was at least a start toward a fucking solution here. Too bad it didn't solve our most basic of problems.

Bastian squeezed my hand in return, leaning in to whisper in my ear, "You're leaving something out, love. I can feel it."

I pulled away from him and gave him an "I'll tell you later" look. Oh, I was leaving a whole host of shit out. Namely, that I had a feeling that Azrael wouldn't help at all, and I'd have to somehow take the damn thing down to the Underworld myself—not that I knew how to get there. Or—and this was a far likelier scenario—Essex was just waiting for us to do this very thing so he could steal the ring and enact whatever plan he had stashed up his sleeve.

Bastian's jaw tightened, his eyes going gold for a moment before fading back to green. Yeah, I wasn't getting anything past him.

"As if he would even help," Darby muttered, resettling on Bishop's lap.

I stood, mirroring Harper as we both stared at Darby. "Then he doesn't help. But you can't keep those souls inside you forever. Because sooner or later Essex is just going to tap you like a keg and suck them out, and then we're just as fucked as we were two damn days ago."

That came out harsher than I'd intended, but it was the truth.

Sensitive to her grief? No.

A truth she needed to hear before she burned from the inside out?

Definitely.

Every part of Darby felt too big, too powerful, too much. And she wasn't holding it together—not that I expected her to, given what she lost—but this wasn't the kind of power you could just let fester.

Darby rose from Bishop's lap, she, Harper, and I an irritated triangle of women. It took me less than a second to realize that if Darby was pissed off enough, she could probably blow me off the map, but I stood firm.

"You know they're right, D," J said from his perch on the floor. He was cuddled up next to the giant Fae I'd met on the battlefield, his injuries all healed up from Darby's overabundance of power. "You can't keep all that bottled up forever. If it doesn't kill your body, it sure as hell will kill your mind."

Darby's smile was rueful, a bitter twist to her lips that was almost a sneer. "You think I don't know that? You think I can't read all your thoughts, feel all your emotions? You think I don't feel your ideas just buzzing in the back of my mind?" She blinked furiously as a tear slipped from her eye. "I know I can't do this forever. I can barely handle today."

"Then what do you plan to do about it?" Thomas asked from his place on the couch, a cut crystal tumbler in his hand that was only half-full of top-shelf whiskey. "Because all I see is a scared child who runs the risk of turning out just like the parents she hates so much." The room was already pretty quiet, but a hush fell over it that added a whole other weight to the air. "If you're the woman I think you are, I would hope the safety of those around you would be your top priority."

Everyone tensed as the tremors that had only occasionally popped up, rumbled through the house hard enough to leave a crack in the living room wall.

"But I suppose choosing to throw a temper tantrum

is more your speed then?" Thomas taunted before sipping his whiskey like he didn't have a care in the world.

"Really?" I squawked. "Antagonizing her? This is your plan?"

Thomas turned his chin to spear me with a bored glare. "It worked on you, didn't it?"

I couldn't recall a time where Thomas' antagonism had done anything but piss me off and confuse the shit out of me, but if it would work on Darby, I wasn't going to complain.

Much.

But Thomas' hard truths had the desired effect as the ground settled. All eyes were on Darby as she gritted her teeth and clenched her fists, her anger held at bay by a wing and a prayer. But soon her hands unclenched, and her jaw relaxed, and she gave Thomas a rueful sort of nod.

"Okay. I will agree something needs to be done, but I don't trust Azrael, and I don't believe Essex, and I don't know what will happen if I extract these souls. So, if we could figure that out, that would be great. In the meantime, I think everyone should head home."

Personally, I thought that was a horrible idea. Leaving her unprotected after Essex had made contact seemed like the worst idea ever. Plus, Bastian and I had been staying in her guestroom, and the fact that she was sending us home rankled a bit. I didn't like the fact that she would be by herself, nor did I like the idea that I might be abandoning her.

When neither bastion nor I moved, Darby pierced us with a glare. "I mean you, too. You've stayed here for two days. I don't need a babysitter anymore."

"The hell you don't," I protested. While everyone else was hurrying to their feet to go, I stayed rooted to the spot. "Essex is still out there—"

"And I've got back up here if he decides to pick a fight. You have a life and a home that doesn't include me. It's about time you went back to it."

It wasn't like I could stay there if she wanted me to go, but I still didn't like it. It felt like I was leaving her to the wolves. "This is a horrible plan you know"

"Probably. But at least my house will be empty."

As someone who hated it when there were far too many people around, I could totally understand. That didn't mean I liked it.

"Fine. But I swear to everything holy, if something happens while I'm gone and you get killed, I am retrieving you from the Underworld and kicking your ass."

Again, not that I knew how to do that, but I'd figure it the fuck out.

"Promises, promises," she muttered, smiling, the pull to her lips just as fake as the mirth in her voice.

This was a horrible idea, but I was going to do it, anyway.

I just hoped it didn't come to bite me in the ass.

9

Upon our reluctant departure from Darby's house, the tense energy coming from Bastian multiplied ten-fold. The entire ride home was filled with tense looks and an even thicker silence, no one saying so much as a peep in the hour-long drive. I knew as soon as we got home, he would ask the questions brewing behind those bottle-green eyes, but I didn't know if I could answer him. He would want to know what I'd been leaving out at Darby's house, and the truth of it would piss him all the way off.

The SUV pulled into the drive, Bastian at the helm. His knuckles were nearly white as he held onto the steering wheel, but he managed to peel them off one by one without ripping the whole thing off Hulk-style.

Everyone else hopped out of the car, but he stayed right where he was, staring at his hands as they fisted on his lap.

Yep, there was no way I was getting out of this interrogation. No way, no how.

The garage door rolled closed, the mechanical clank of it locking almost making me jump out of my skin. Then he rotated in his seat to stare at me. "Well, love, I'm all ears."

Oh, so we're doing this here then. Super.

Rather than answer him, I got out of the car and headed for the garage door. I didn't make it two steps past the SUV before my back was pressed into the still-cooling metal, and he was in my space, pressing his big body into me.

"I don't know if this has escaped your attention, but I wasn't asking." Bastian's expression was cool and calculating, but I saw the worry and fear and bitter agony behind the mask. It tempered all my resistance, leaving me with coy sass rather than unmitigated rage at being pinned down.

"Enlighten me then. What do you want to know?" It was a stupid question, sure. I knew the answer, but stalling seemed like my best course of action.

"I want to know what you're hiding. I want to know what you didn't say at Darby's house. I want to know why you think not telling me is a good idea. When has keeping the other person in the dark ever worked out for us?"

His fingers curled around the back of my neck as he tilted my head up so I could not escape his gaze as it dropped to my lips. "And I want to know why you don't want to tell me."

The heat of him radiated through my body, and it warmed a part of me that had been cold since seeing that stupid note. As high-handed as it was, it still made me feel protected, which was stupid and girly and... "You know the answer to that. You're going to freak out, and then I'm going to freak out, and then it's going to turn into a big, huge mess that I can't fix when I already have a pile of messes that I can't fix in my back pocket. I just wanted five minutes where nobody expected me to fix their problems."

He dipped his nose so it brushed mine. "No one expects you to fix everything. Especially not me. Now, tell me what is going on."

I sighed, basking in his heat for a moment before I broke everything. "You're going to freak out."

"Then I'll freak out. And then after that, we'll deal with it together."

I shook my head, breaking the tense stare-down and thought long and hard about how I could tell him the truth. Swallowing thickly, I let it all out. "Azrael isn't going to help. And she can't keep those souls inside her. They have to be brought to the Underworld, and if Azrael isn't going to help, the only person I could think to take them—is me." I flicked my gaze back to him, and almost wished I hadn't.

The change that came over him was immediate. His eyes flashed gold, the burning orbs boring a hole into my soul.

"No," he whispered with a vehemence that shook me to my core.

"What do you mean no? There isn't anyone else—"

He pressed further into me. "It is not going to be you."

I broke our stare-down, my eyes falling to his lips, his jaw—anything but his eyes. Those eyes were breaking me, and I didn't know I could be more broken than I already was. "It has to be me. There is no one else."

His grip tightened on the back of my neck, his fingers threading into my hair as his other arm banded around my back. I had no other choice but to look at him, no other choice but to hear him. "You barely survived the In-Between."

"No, *you* barely survived the In-Between. I just got

stuck is all." Really, it was semantics at this point, but the argument needed to be made.

Inexplicably, he somehow invaded even more of my space, pressing harder into me. "You're not leaving me, do you understand? I don't care about this world. I don't care if everything falls apart. You are not leaving me alone to live without you. Until the world stops turning and the sun stops burning, remember?"

I wanted to be mad, I really did. But all I felt was heat, his warmth, his soul boring into me. "But—"

"But, nothing. You are not leaving me behind. You're not doing this by yourself. I won't let you leave me. Not when I've just found you. Not when—" His sentence broke off as if he couldn't say another word. Instead, he dropped his lips to mine in a hard, fierce kiss.

I couldn't say why the almost violent touch of his mouth to mine relieved me, but it did. The fear, the fury, the uncertainty faded away once his lips made contact. The rough burr of his stubble against my hand as I cupped his face sent shivers down my spine. Bastian's hold on me got tighter, and he lifted me off my feet, bracing the both of us against the SUV as our kiss consumed us.

Three days.

It had only been three days since I'd lost him.

Three days since I'd searched the In-Between in the hopes of finding him. Three days since his breathing stopped, and he whispered how much he loved me as he faded away. He couldn't live this life without me? Well, I couldn't do it without him, either.

I couldn't walk this road by myself, always wondering if he was going to… to…

Every bit of it came crashing down on me all at once. What we'd survived, what I'd lost, what could be in my future if the worst were to happen and I lost him again. Because there would be a time when I wouldn't be able to call him back, when I wouldn't be able to save him.

When I would be alone, too.

Bastian readjusted his grip, his fingers fumbling with the fly of my jeans, and I dropped biting kisses to his jaw, his neck. My fangs ached in my mouth, practically begging to tear into his flesh, but I held back. At the touch of my fangs against his neck, he groaned, his large fingers hooking in the waist of my jeans and yanking. I felt more than heard the button ping to the ground as the zipper ripped apart.

I wanted him out of those clothes. I wanted his skin on mine—his blood in my mouth. My hands roamed, yanking up his shirt so I could feel every part of him I could reach. And then I was on my feet, my front pressed against the side of the truck as he roughly shoved my jeans to my knees, the cool air kissing my skin just as he had been a moment before. A second later—though it felt like an eternity—his warmth returned as he snaked his hand up my shirt. Tugging my bra out of the way, he cupped my breast with one hand as he notched himself at my opening with the other.

"Promise me," he growled in my ear. "Promise you aren't going without me."

I rocked back, aching to take him inside of me, but his grip tightened, stilling my hips.

"Please," I begged, tipping my head back to rest it on his shoulder. Everything ached, my heart, my sex, my fangs.

"Promise me, and I will. I'll give you everything. Just promise me."

And I was supposed to say no to this how again?

"I promise," I breathed, and he pushed inside, filling me in one stroke.

His other hand collared around my neck, directing my chin so he could press hot, fevered kisses to my lips as he moved in the most delicious rhythm. It was angry and hurried and so fucking beautiful, my heart felt like it was too big for my chest. I moaned into his mouth, and he groaned into mine. I didn't care where we were or who could walk in and see us. It was as if there was no one else on the planet but us.

Without warning he pulled out, and I moaned at the loss until I felt him yank my jeans the rest of the way off. Maybe he tore them off—I didn't know, nor did I care. Then he spun me, hauling me up his body so he could fill me again. The heat of his body hit my front in an almost blistering way, and I couldn't deny the ache in my fangs another second. I tightened my legs around his hips, tore his shirt over the top of his head, and struck. The thick, decadent lifeblood gushed into my mouth as his strokes got rougher, more needy, more desperate.

I fucking loved it.

One swallow, and I felt every kiss he'd ever thought of pressing to my skin. Two swallows, and I experienced every lick he'd wanted, everywhere he wanted to taste me. Three, and my climax raced toward me, the pleasure barreling into me with the force of a freight train. Pulling my fangs from his skin, the moan that came out of me could probably wake the dead. Tingles raced up my legs all the way to my scalp as Bastian thrust his fingers in my hair and jerked my mouth to his in another blistering kiss. A moment later he groaned out his own climax, and I swallowed that down, too.

Our heavy breaths mingled as we rested our now-sweaty foreheads together. My brain was officially scrambled, but I did gather that I was indeed naked from the waist down in the garage with what was probably my ass print on the side of the truck. Also? My pants were probably toast.

I mentally shrugged. *Totally worth it.*

Smiling, Bastian pressed another kiss to my lips before easing out of me and setting me on my feet. We located the remnants of my jeans and underwear, which turned out, wouldn't work to cover my ass in any sort of way. Hell, I'd wondered how he'd gotten them over my boots, I just hadn't figured he'd ripped them apart completely. Bastian reached behind his neck and yanked his black T-shirt the rest of the way off, handing it over. Surprisingly, I hadn't ripped it to shreds. I slipped off my T-shirt and dropped his over my head. The hem hit about mid-thigh, which would have to do.

Bastian tugged me behind him, checking that the coast was clear before leading us out of the garage and to what I now thought of as our room. We showered together, washing away the day's grief and our doubts, and we didn't talk again about the plan in my head that would most certainly fail.

We lived in that happy bubble for a little while.

And then it came crashing down on us.

10

"Please tell me you're kidding," Emrys breathed, sitting back in her chair like my stupidity was contagious.

I just held Bastian's hand tighter and shook my head. We were in her office, sitting in the very chairs where I had fed from Bastian for the first time. My fingers traced the crescent tears in the leather as I held back a smile. "I'm not, and if you'd have seen it, you wouldn't be kidding, either."

"I saw enough up at the lake to know you're dealing with complex magic that you have no idea how to harness. You want me to be pulling those souls out of her? Me and what bleeding army?"

It was cute that she honestly thought that I believed

she was some fragile little thing. "Oh, please. You could probably do this in your sleep. Quit playing with me."

Normally, I'd be a little scared of Emrys. She was my boss, a badass druid, and had just a tad too much of gray in her soul to keep me on my toes. But my sister was rocking and rolling the planet for fuck's sake. I didn't have time to be afraid of Emrys.

I had bigger fish to fry.

"Contrary to popular belief, lass, I am not the end all be all of magical power. What was done to that girl took a whole coven of witches. I alone am no coven." Emrys steepled her fingers like the conversation was over and she'd delivered the final blow.

"So, you're telling me that you, plus Simon, Bastian, Bishop, and Dahlia—plus whatever mojo that Fae, Jimmy has—can't compete with a coven of witches half of ya'll's ages? And mind you, I'm being nice with that estimate since I know you and Thomas are older than Jesus himself. Go ahead and pull the other leg while you're at it."

She sat back, a ghost of a smile crossing her lips before the seriousness returned, her odd reddish eyes flashing with warning. "I'm not pulling your leg. I'm telling you the facts. The fact is that without Azrael's help I don't think we can pull those souls from her. And more than that, I think if we try, it could kill her."

Risking Darby's life wasn't something I was too keen on doing, but I feared waiting wasn't a better option, either.

"Then we need Azrael's help," I conceded, throwing my hands up. "She can't stand that much power inside her, she's a hair's breadth from losing her fucking mind. So, if we need to summon him, or lasso him, or what the fuck ever, it needs to get done. Bishop called me at eight this morning to tell me how she had destroyed her whole kitchen. There's only so much she can annihilate before it starts actually obliterating her life."

I felt the swish of wings a moment before my father spoke, his appearance making both Bastian and Emrys nearly jump out of their skin.

"You called?" Azrael asked from the doorway.

I tossed an irritated glare over my shoulder. "Yeah, I did. Lots. Good of you to show up."

Bastian found my hand and squeezed my fingers, likely trying to get me to shut up. But he didn't realize just how many times I had pleaded in my head for Azrael to help. Hundreds, maybe thousands of times over the last two days and he'd stayed gone. When our brother showed up, when that stupid note was in the grass, when Darby was breaking her living room apart.

I had begged and pleaded with him to come and help us—help her—and still he'd stayed away.

"Sorry," he said, tilting his dark head to the side as he assessed Bastian. "I was working."

He and I both knew he could do his job from anywhere. In fact, he had done this job from a squat prison underneath thousands of pounds of rock and rubble and water where he'd stayed for close to twenty years. And now when we needed him that's when he decided he needed to be on site to collect souls?

I call bullshit.

Azrael's eyes flashed purple for a moment before they hid behind his usual glamour of dark brown. "Collecting souls is not my only job. You'd know that if you had taken me up on my offer to teach you. Instead, you decided to stay for *love*."

He rolled his eyes in derision, but I knew it was fake. Azrael might not have known real love like what I had, but he knew enough to worry about his kids. Knew enough to not force me to come to heel. He knew enough to send me back to Bastian when I'd been stuck in the In-Between.

Stop trying to make us hate you. You might be a dick, but you aren't a monster. You know what love is, I don't care how old and jaded you are.

Both Bastian and Emrys stood, the pair of them bowing at the waist in deference to my father. Sure, he was the Angel of Death, but bowing? The act seemed to make Azrael uncomfortable, and so did the silence that hung in the room.

Rolling my eyes, I stood and introduced my boss and my... Bastian.

"Azrael, meet Emrys Zane and Sebastian Cartwright." I carefully left off who these people were to me, but since my father could read my mind, it was really unnecessary.

"A pleasure," Azrael said, nodding to them both. "I understand that Darby isn't handling things very well."

Well, that is the understatement of the fucking century. Good of you to finally give a damn.

Was antagonizing the Angel of Death a smart play? Probably not.

Was it exactly what he deserved for being the vaguest parent known to mankind? Absolutely.

Azrael speared me with a glare but continued like he hadn't heard me mentally berating him. "I would like to help. I believe with your assistance I may be able to extract the souls that Mariana has trapped inside Darby."

That was code for "I let Darby absorb those souls

because I was too chickenshit to go up against the woman who stole my ring, put me in that prison cell, and dumped a couple kilotons of rock, rubble, and lake water on top." Darby had told me what that ring had showed her, and the fact of the matter was, was that all of this could have been avoided if Azrael had ever—just once—fought back. He let this happen, let this bullshit unfold because… because I had no idea why. And now he wanted help?

Of course he did. And we'd accept it because there was no other way, and he'd learn exactly fuck all from this experience except that he could get away with doing whatever the hell he wanted to do and fuck the rest of us.

"You know, you and your brother think quite alike," Azrael murmured, spearing me with a look of wrath. "Blaming me for the things I *had* to do. You don't see me doing that to you."

Without much thought, I was on my feet and in his face. "That's because it's your fault, you fuck. *You're* the reason I had to do those things. *You're* the reason I'm here. *You're* the reason I turned into a monster. You did this, fucking around with arcane women who had no idea what a curse being your child would be, and then you leave them holding the bag. Then you come back into our lives like you're some benevolent savior when it's your fault our lives are shit in the first fucking place. Get fucked, you asshole."

My lip curled on its very own and I contemplated spitting right in his face. Instead, I whispered the truth. "Your son killed my parents, he killed me, and then he had his minion kill the very last person on this planet that gave a shit about me. You have no right to come into this house and insult me like that. No. Right. I don't care whether you're a god or not."

That's when I realized I was looking Azrael in the eye—like *right* in the eye. I had totally meant to get in his face, but not like this. Azrael was tall—taller than even Axel, who had to be six and a half feet of ghoul giant. Looking down, I quickly understood what had given me the boost.

My feet were dangling a foot over the plush carpet. I was floating.

I.

Was.

Floating.

In the air. I was floating in the air like someone had shoved a helium tank up my butt and cranked the lever wide. Okay, so that was a gross analogy, but the imagery still worked.

And Azrael?

Well, he had a cat that ate the canary smile like

everything was going according to plan. Naturally, it pissed me off and made me forget for a second that I was essentially flying. Okay, so not exactly flying, but *Peter Pan* had nothing on this shit.

"What the fuck are you smiling at?"

His hands rose, and he pressed them to the top of my shoulders, resetting my feet back on the floor. "Not a thing, kid. Not a thing."

Jerk.

"Next thing you know," Azrael said, chuckling, "you'll be sprouting wings like your dear old dad, and then we'll really be in trouble."

"Can we get back to the task at hand already?" I muttered, not even looking at Bastian or Emrys, and sort of thankful it was them and not Harper who saw this whole thing. She would have shouted the house down, made a whole scene, and then I'd never live it down.

Azrael opened his mouth to say something—likely to give me more shit if I were to guess—when the whole house rocked under my feet. Books rattled off the shelves and the lights flickered.

"Well, fuck," my father groaned, his hair turning white and his wings coming out in full force. "I thought we had more time."

Time? Time for what?

An instant later, Bishop La Roux appeared in Emrys' office, bypassing every ward and magical protection we had on the place. In his arms was a seizing Darby, her body shaking in time with the tremors of the house. Only, the house wasn't going to withstand the onslaught. The hardwood floor splintered under my feet, knocking me to the unstable ground. Bastian grabbed me by the waist, pulling me up with a rough tug.

"Outside," he shouted. "Everyone outside!"

Bishop and my wayward father disappeared, taking Darby with them. As we ran from the room, light fixtures swayed before breaking from their fastenings and falling to the floor. Books toppled from their shelves, art slipped and fell from their nails. Harper screeched in Axel's arms—the big man held her like a football tucked under his arm as he sprinted down the stairs. Simon protected Dahlia with a silver tray that he had picked up from who knew where, and Thomas had ahold of Clem and Emrys, dragging them from the house with a speed I almost couldn't track through the shattered French doors, with us hot on his heels.

And then we were outside, slipping in the wet grass as we tried to get away from the house. Too bad the outside wasn't much better. The ground pitched and rolled, great fissures in the earth cracked wide open, threatening to swallow us whole. We converged on Bishop, my still-seizing sister, and Azrael in full Angel of Death mode, his wings spread wide and his eyes flashing purple for all the world to see.

"We can't wait," Azrael ordered. "We have to do this now."

11

We have to do this now.

That was all well and good, but I didn't have that first clue as to what we were doing, or how we were supposed to pull the souls from Darby, or keep her alive once we did. I was still having trouble standing up for fuck's sake. The ground was still bucking in time with Darby's convulsions, the soil cracking under our feet with each shake.

The thing that made my heart sink and gut go into freefall? I wasn't sure she was breathing. Darby's lips had an unhealthy blue tint that spoke of a solid lack of oxygen. I wasn't like her. I couldn't give away power or save people from the brink of death. I felt useless and impotent and...

But Azrael sure as hell seemed to know what he was doing. He gave Dahlia and Emrys a nod, crooking his finger as the three of them surrounded Bishop and Darby, latching their hands together. Bishop clutched Darby close to his chest, shaking his head like he was having an internal debate.

"You have to. If you're in there with her, you won't make it. You want my daughter to blame herself more than she already does?" Azrael growled, his purple eyes flashing. "Let her go."

Bishop squeezed Darby once more before he gently placed her on the quaking ground and crawled from the circle like he was walking to the gallows.

"Sloane," Azrael called. "Get that ring off her thumb. Hold it in your hand and stand beside her."

I moved to do as told—shocker, I know—when Bastian latched onto my upper arm and drew me back. "You just told us whoever is in that circle with Darby will die, or was that bullshit?"

Azrael rolled his eyes before spearing Bastian with a violent purple glare. "But Sloane isn't alive, now, is she? Any other objections? I only have a child dying right before my eyes."

Bastian's grip loosened, and I tossed what I hoped was a reassuring glance over my shoulder as I shakily made my way to Darby's side. Prying the obsidian ring off her cold thumb, I held it in my hands and raised them to Azrael.

"Keep holding it, and don't move."

Well, that sounds ominous.

And it sounded like a whole lot of "not a good idea," too, but I kept that to myself and held still. I felt the power crackle on the air before the first zing of a soul hit the ring in my hand. A blindingly bright light nearly seared my retinas as the soul circled the cool metal in my hand, swirling like a tornado before it winked out of sight. The metal warmed slightly as it absorbed the soul, the ring rocking in my palm before it settled again.

What I thought was funny—not in a funny "Ha-ha" way and more "WTF" with a side of "Holy shit"—was that this was one single soul, and by my calculations, there were about a hundred thousand more coming. I met Azrael's eyes. His brow furrowed with concentration, his irises blazed violet, glowing just like one of those souls. But the sweat on his brow and slight ration of fear in his gaze was what made my whole stomach sink into the ground. Mariana's spell—even after her death—was too damn strong. Too strong for a fucking death deity.

Oh, shit. Oh, fuck, oh, shit, oh, no.

"Bishop, Simon, Bastian, get over here," Azrael ordered, and the men raced for him, joining Emrys and Dahlia in this macabre circle.

As soon as the guys joined the circle, the heat of the ring in my hand went from simply hot to raging inferno levels. Darby shook once more before her whole body lifted off the ground, the earth stilling as she bowed like she was being broken in half. Then she let out a scream that would haunt me until I was gone from this earth. Her eyes opened, the blazing white light of thousands of souls erupting from her lids as a scalding beam broke from her chest.

A gale-force wind tore through the air, nearly knocking us all off our feet, but I managed to stay right there—right next to Darby. Fire sprung up in a circle around both Darby and I, cutting us off from the rest, as lightning crackled through the sky. Then it was as if the heavens broke. Rain poured down on us, and all the while, Darby screamed as she hovered over the ground, the souls pouring from her chest like a dam breaking.

Then those souls reached for the ring, the brilliant tornado of thousands of trapped spirits whipped around the warming metal. And then I was the one screaming. Each soul warmed the metal, each one raising the temperature of the ring ten-fold, until it was glowing white and burning the flesh from my hands.

I wanted to drop it. Wanted to throw it away or chuck it into the darkest, deepest volcano. But Azrael had told me to stay still, so for Darby, I did. Tears streamed down my face as the blistering agony raced through my body, the tremors of pain rocking me to my core. The light in my palm suddenly died, and along with it, Darby's limp form slammed back onto the ground. The ring of fire petered out, the rains dousing it as if it were all meant to be. Blinding pain shuddered through me as I knelt on the soggy grass.

My limbs refused to obey my commands as I stared in horror at the monstrosity in my palms. What had been an obsidian ring was now a trio of metallic sigils burned into the skin of my hands. The metal and stone had burned away, and now all I was left with was the growing horror that someone had played a horrible trick on me.

"What did you do?" I whispered, still staring at the three markings, each one I recognized from the In-Between. They had been on the blue door that had led me out and back to Bastian. "What did you do?" I asked again, louder this time as realization dawned.

Those souls had been in Darby and now... now they were in me.

The silence from Azrael was telling, and I tore my gaze from my hands to spear my father with a pleading stare.

"What did you do?" I whimpered, tears clogging my throat.

Sorrow and what I could only assume was pity raced across his features. "What had to be done. Gather yourself. We leave in an hour." Then that bastard winked out of sight, leaving me with a cryptic pronouncement and a boatload of agony.

The silence from everyone was more telling than anything else, each of their quiet stares full of pity. Maybe they knew what was going on. Maybe they knew why Azrael had done what he had, but I sure as fuck didn't. Bastian broke from the circle first, his rough hands cupping my cheeks as he knelt in front of me, his bottle-green eyes boring holes in me.

He knew what was going on. He had to know. Didn't he?

"Sloane? Love?" *Are you all right?* That last bit sounded like a gong in my head, even though his lips hadn't moved.

I couldn't speak, the tears clogging my throat as a wave of helplessness pulled me under. Was I all right? No, I could honestly say I was not.

"Sloane?" a voice croaked from behind me, and I

turned to see an incredibly pale Darby sitting up, as if the act was the most torturous thing she had ever done in her entire life. Hell, if Bishop hadn't been helping her, I doubted she would have made it vertical. "What —what happened?" Her gaze flicked from my face to my hands to the open yard around us, the ground still marred with deep cracks and burnt grass. Then they fell on my hands again, Azrael's sigils burned into my palms taking the sole of her focus.

"Oh, no," she whispered, her eyes welling with tears. "What did he do?"

That was the question for the ages, and one no one had deigned to answer.

Shrugging, I shoved every bit of pain and worry down deep where it wouldn't bubble up my throat and choke me. "He didn't say."

He had, however, mentioned something about us leaving in an hour, and I had no idea what "gathering myself" meant.

None of this was going to plan—not that my plan was fleshed out exactly—but this was so far out of my scope, I practically had whiplash with how fast everything had turned. Bastian cupped my cheeks in his hands, the warmth a comfort in the midst of all this uncertainty. His expression had a healthy dose of fear and not a little bit of trepidation.

How do I tell her? His thoughts sounded in my brain. And then the truth unfolded inside his mind, showing me all the things Azrael hadn't meant him to see while they were connected in the circle.

We weren't just leaving the house in an hour—oh, no. We were leaving this plane of existence altogether. Azrael intended to take me to the Underworld. And that hour time frame he'd given me to prepare myself?

That was the best-case scenario.

"No." As far as answers went, it fit the bill, but it didn't quite cut it when it came to explaining all the reasons why going to the Underworld was a terrible, no-good idea for someone like me. All the fears that I'd shoved down slammed into me in a wave, threatening to yank me under.

When I'd originally had the idea, it hadn't actually been real for me. I knew it was a possibility that I would have to go there, but—

"I'm going with you," Bastian growled, the tips of his fingers pressing into my scalp as he held my head in his hands. "You promised me, Sloane. Remember? You swore."

"What?" Simon breathed from behind him, and then he charged forward, ripping Bastian away from me and hauling him to his feet. A blackness settled over Simon's irises and sclera—the effect practically demonic as the smaller death mage lost hold on his rage. "Are you crazy? Is that it? Kick over and leave me behind? I don't bloody think so."

Darby had explained Azrael's decree after her father had died. That someone who had been brought back couldn't come back twice. That there was nothing he could do—that there was no way for Killian to return to the living a second time.

I'd promised Bastian I'd take him with me, essentially killing him and selfishly separating him from his only living family. I really was a monster, wasn't I?

"Stay out of this, Simon. You know damn well you'd do the same for Dahlia. And there's no proof that arcaners have that same rule applied to them. I'm going, brother, and there is nothing you could say to stop me."

Thomas roughly pulled the brothers apart, shaking them both like he was trying to knock some sense into them. "Want to clue the rest of us in? Not everyone mind-melded with a death god for fuck's sake."

"Azrael is taking Sloane to the Underworld," Simon answered, his face twisted in derision. "My idiot brother wants to go with her, even though he most likely will be trapped down there." He tore Thomas' hand off his flannel shirt and shoved Bastian's shoulder, adding a little of his power behind it so Bastian stumbled. "You promised me when Mum and Dad died that you wouldn't follow them. You're a liar, brother." Simon pointed a finger right at Bastian's face, a black swirl of magic racing up his arm. "You're a fucking liar."

Bastian pinched his brow as his shoulders hunched. "I made that promise when we were children, Simon. Tell me. If Dahlia were in the same position, would you let her go alone, knowing that she might be trapped there, too? Would you kiss her on the lips and bid her goodbye, knowing she might not come back to you? Or would you follow her and damn the consequences? Because living another thousand years without her would be the worst torture you could imagine?"

Simon looked like Bastian had slapped him right across the face, an expression that turned pained when Dahlia threaded her fingers through his. His gaze broke from his brother's, and he stared down into her whiskey-colored eyes, his pooling with tears as reality set in.

"It's not fair," he whispered.

Dahlia smiled at him, a sweet bitter smile that spoke of her own pain. "It never is."

"Why?" Darby whispered, still staring at my rapidly healing hands, the metallic sigils becoming permanent fixtures in my flesh. "Why would he do this to you? After all you've lost."

That I couldn't answer—not really. I got flashes of it in Bastian's brain, but I didn't understand.

I wasn't sure I ever would.

12

Simon wiped at his leaking eyes before striding across the grass and pulling me up by my biceps. "He gave you an hour and we've wasted enough of it. You have to get ready."

Dumbstruck, I allowed him to pull me by the forearm back to the house. How did one get ready for a trek to the Underworld? Was I supposed to load up with weapons? Did I need a sword? Did guns work down there?

"Clem, get their leathers ready," he called over his shoulder as we crunched over broken glass and fallen books.

The house looked no better than it had a week ago after our little invasion, and I had to wonder how many times it had broken apart and been put back together by magic over the years. Simon muttered to himself for a second before picking through the debris, yanking me behind him to the staircase. An irritated trill pulled my gaze to my feet, and an angry set of glowing green eyes pierced me with an annoyed glare. Simon yanked me again, and Isis wound around his feet, almost tripping him.

"Damn and blast, Isis. It's not my fault you went and hid under the bed. The whole bloody house was going to fall on us, you mangy feline, and you can't die."

She couldn't? Well, that was new information—and sort of comforting if I was being honest. The world without a little skeleton kitty in it seemed just a bit awful to me. I pulled my arm out of Simon's hold and picked up the bone cat, cuddling her in my arms as I continued following him up the stairs.

"Did evil Simon leave you behind, my sweet girl? What a bad daddy." Scratching at her nonexistent fur, I smiled evilly when Simon shot me a look over his shoulder as he muttered something about children these days.

Children? Pfft.

Considering Simon looked and acted younger than quite a few of my classmates when I was actually in college, he had little to no room to talk, but I didn't say that out loud. We entered Simon's domain, and he twisted his wrist before snapping the fingers of his right hand. Candles on the dusty surfaces flared to life, somehow not toppled in the commotion. Simon pressed on a wooden panel, and much like Emrys' office, the panel swung inward to reveal a whole other room.

This room was lit, too, with half-burnt black candles, their wax pooling on the stone floor. As soon as I crossed the threshold from Simon's room into this new place, the chill of the air had me shivering around Isis.

"Simon?"

I wanted to ask where we were. I wanted him to tell me a happy lie, but I knew as soon as I crossed into this new room, that we weren't in the house anymore. I hugged Isis tighter before setting her at my feet, the unease in my gut pulling me back toward the open door.

"Oh, stop it," he chided, not even bothering to turn around from his inspection of a massive shelf with dusty bottles and even dustier books. "If I wanted to brick you in the wine cellar, I'd have been more creative about it."

"Referencing Poe isn't making me feel any better, you know."

Simon shot an equally evil smile over his shoulder as his fingers perused the shelf by feel alone, pulling a huge tome into his arms without even bothering to look at the title. "That's what you get for agreeing to take my brother to his probable death. Now, do you want him to come back with you or do you want him stuck there? Because if you answer wrong, I really will brick you in the wine cellar. Just so we're clear."

My whole body practically wilted into the stone floor. "You can do that? You can…"

I wanted to cry I was so happy, the relief hitting me square in the chest.

"I believe so, but we don't have time to dally. And…" Simon winced as he trailed off. "You're going to need to lose a toe. It should grow back almost instantly, but yeah."

"What?"

"Normally it would be fingers, but those take longer to grow back, and we don't have that kind of time. The toe will just have to do. Though, it will give you less time to work with."

"Better make it three," Thomas insisted, filling the doorway. "Axel and I are coming, too."

I scoffed, staring at Thomas like he'd lost a head. "I'm not losing three toes. One for Bastian, sure, but you two? Hell no. And why—"

"We're coming, girlie," Axel said from behind him, shouldering through the doorway like the giant he was. "Emrys informed us of Azrael's real reason for getting those souls out of Darby all quick like. Essex is coming for you both, kid, and I'm not forgetting what I promised you. I owe you and yours for what you did. Not to mention, Darby's the reason I never have to look at my murdering father ever again. I ain't leaving ya'll unprotected. No way, no how. So, cough up some toes."

With everything that had happened over the last few days, I'd forgotten that the leader of the Monroe nest had been Axel's dad. With that added wrinkle, there was no way either of these idiots were going to let Bastian and I go to the Underworld—of all places —alone.

Ugh. Fine.

Bile rose in my throat as I started unlacing my boots. "Left or right foot?"

Was I really going to do this? Like for real? Just cough up some toes for Simon to use in some weird death mage woo-woo, no questions asked?

Evidently, I was.

"You're left-handed, correct?" Simon asked as he lifted a gleaming cleaver off a dusty table, littered with candles and an honest-to-god shrunken head and a mummified bird of some kind.

My stomach dipped and I took a step back. "Yeah?"

"The right will do."

I'd been half-joking when I'd asked, but Simon was serious, his normally jovial expression dialed to cold, calculating awful. Perfect.

"Hold her."

Then Axel and Thomas had ahold of my arms as Simon knelt at my right foot and brought the cleaver down.

Funnily enough, I didn't feel it at first. The blade was so sharp, it was a simple breeze against my flesh, and really, considering what I'd just gone through, I kind of figured I was due a lucky break.

As it turned out, the sharper the blade, the longer it took to hurt. About two seconds later the pain hit, and the howl that came out of my mouth scared the shit out of even me. My legs buckled, Thomas and Axel taking the bulk of my weight as they eased me to the ground. Simon buggered off to go do whatever spell he had dreamt up in his fool skull, and I cussed a blue streak as the pain subsided enough for me to actually form words.

"You son of a cunt-bag motherfucker. You piece of rancid gutter shit. *Fuck* you."

Then for the second time in my life, I puked on Thomas' boots.

I'd love to say I managed to hold it together after that, but after I emptied about a pint of blood and Clem's famous chicken and dumplings on Thomas' handcrafted Italian leather boots, I went ahead and passed out. Really, that was fair. I'd sort of had a rough day, and as soon as Azrael got back, it was about to get a whole lot worse. I figured I was due a little gastrointestinal pyrotechnics.

Thomas didn't think this was at all funny, but I woke up from my little snooze to the roar of Axel and Simon's laughter. Simon himself was laughing as he weaved a fair bit of dark magic, the swirls of his power coiling like snakes up his arms.

"That is two pairs of boots she's ruined in a month. Not even a month. A week!"

I knew Thomas was a vain bastard, but I'd just sacrificed a toe so *he* could help *me* out. I deserved some slack. And no one told him to throw me off a water tower. That was *his* fault.

"Aww, come on, Thomas." Axel chuckled as he strapped blades and other such weapons into the pockets of a rather nifty cargo vest. "Don't you remember the last time you lost a limb? No one is holding onto their lunch. Not even you."

"And the water tower incident was your fault," I croaked. "You know I'm afraid of heights."

Thomas shot me a glare, his jade eyes glittering with wrath. Yeah, if we survived this, he was going to make me pay for that, and probably not with money— not that I had any. Clem breezed into the room with an armload of leathers and a pair of boots. She handed off the boots to Thomas without so much as a word before kneeling to pass me the leathers.

I hadn't paid that much attention to Clem over the last couple of days, but the redheaded revenant seemed less bubbly than usual. Her odd gray skin and red hair appeared duller than the norm, and her smile—not that I thought this was a happy time or anything—was gone. Even in the height of battle when she was wielding her favorite shotgun, she'd been smiling. It had only been since Simon had died and come back that she'd been this way.

"Hiya, Sloane," she whispered.

"Clem."

"I cleaned the blood from the battle out of the stitching, and I had Emrys beef up the protection magic. Bastian is coming with your weapons and such."

I reached out a hand to her shoulder, the cool temp of her skin startling me just a bit. Clementine was the only revenant I knew of, so I didn't know if the cold skin was a problem or not, but I was worried. *Or I was using her as an excuse to not think about traversing the Underworld with the love of my life and my sperm donor.*

You know, *whatever.*

"You okay?" Stupid question, right? But it was all I had.

She blinked at me before her gaze went to Simon and returned to me. "He'll be okay, you know. If you and Bastian don't come back. Dahlia and me and the gang will make sure of it. But Bastian? He won't be okay without you. So if it comes down to it—and you want to choose saving him instead of keeping your promise—I'd keep the promise."

A tear leaked out of my eye before I could hold it back. Wiping it away, I muttered, "Did Bastian tell you to tell me that?"

She shook her head. "I've been with those boys for eighty years. I know them better than I knew my own flesh and blood when I was alive. There's nothing I don't know about them. Simon? He's a survivor—always has been. Bastian? He does everything for love. Love of his family, love of his brother, the Night Watch, as rag-tag a bunch as we are. I've never seen him like this before. If you left, you'd take his heart with you."

There was nothing I could say to rebut that, so I

simply nodded. She helped me hobble back out of Simon's dungeon lair and into his room, assisting me in the rather awkward clothing removal as I tried to balance while still regrowing toes. Truth be told, if the initial pain and the unbearable itch of them regrowing wasn't so horrendous, I might not have minded so much.

Okay, so that was a total lie. I minded. A lot. But if it meant Bastian could come out of this unscathed? I would lose a thousand toes. Though, I really didn't want to think about what Simon needed those toes for or what Bastian, Thomas, and Axel were about to consume.

Nope. Don't go there. That way lies up-chucking.

By the time Clem helped me wriggle into my leathers, my toes were all grown back except for the nails. Also, toes without nails? Supreme grossness.

So long, open-toed sandals. I'll miss you.

I had just tied the laces of my boots when Bastian poked his head around the screen. Once I could stand on my own, Clem had left me to dress myself, so it was just me, him, and a boatload of silence behind a dressing screen.

"Thomas and Axel talk to you?"

If he meant did they hold me down while Simon procured spell ingredients? Then sure. "Yep."

"You didn't talk them out of it?"

I almost laughed but couldn't quite manage it. "Was I supposed to? I was kind of under the impression the only way I was going to talk them out of it was to behead them. Seemed better to have them watch our backs, don't you think?"

But I had a feeling—no matter what pretty words I used to dress it up—that I was signing their death warrants, anyway.

Bastian must have seen as much on my face because he crowded me—like he was prone to do—and cupped my cheeks in his hands.

"We'll make it out of this, love," he whispered before dropping a soul-searing kiss on my lips. Letting myself fall into that kiss, I could almost believe him.

Almost.

13

"**H**er toes, Simon?" Bastian yelled as he tried to shove me behind him. He had just learned of his brother's newfangled spell ingredients, and it was safe to say he wasn't pleased. "Plural?"

Simon rolled his eyes as he strained a viscous liquid into three glass vials. "She's fine. Do you want to come back to the land of the living or not? No offense or anything, but I wouldn't want to go into the Underworld without backup. It was three measly toes, and they grew back in ten minutes."

I winced. Those measly toes had been missed. "I volunteered, Bastian."

Would I have rather *not* lost the three largest toes on my right foot? Absolutely.

Did I regret it? Time would tell.

But I didn't want the brothers fighting—especially not right now. Not when we were so close to leaving. Every moment that passed, I braced myself for an attack—the whispers of Essex's return threatening each breath that gusted through my lips.

Simon completed his concoction and fit a cork stopper in each vial before threading a leather cord around the spout. Passing the vials off, he immediately smacked Axel, who seemed ready to unstop the bottle and drink the contents.

"Honestly, Axel? I know you're a ghoul, and cannibalism is your thing, but..." Simon trailed off, giving a full-body shiver. "It's not for drinking. It's for wearing, you idiot."

Axel leveled him with a scowl. "Well, how was I supposed to know? You just gave me food. I thought I was supposed to eat it."

My stomach lurched at the idea of Axel chowing down on flesh. "You haven't..." I couldn't think of the right way to ask. Aunt Julie had been just chilling in his giant walk-in refrigerator for months now, and even though I hadn't thought of how I wanted to honor her passing, Axel using her as an appetizer was just wrong.

Axel seemed embarrassed but also like he knew what I was going to ask. "No, I haven't been snacking on your aunt, Sloane. Not only would that be wrong on all kinds of levels, but I also prefer, umm... fresh meat."

I was in serious danger of puking on Thomas' boots again, but the fact that Julie's remains were safe did fill me with a bit of hope.

"Wear them. Don't let them break," Simon instructed. "The whole point is to make the Underworld believe you're supposed to be there, so it doesn't kick you out or try to kill you to make you stay. Since Sloane is already dead, the tincture in that vial should mask you at least for a little while."

Bastian reluctantly looped the bottle around his neck, tucking it under his body armor to keep it safe.

"But," he continued, "time works differently down there. A day in the Underworld would be just a few moments up here. These vials will get you a day, tops. Any longer, and I can't promise the efficacy."

I took a moment to digest that bit of knowledge. I knew we were under a time crunch, but now with the added stakes of Simon's potion not working, I felt more than a little uneasy.

"And here I thought I was just taking my daughter to the Underworld," Azrael muttered as he breezed through Simon's dungeon lair without so much as a "How do you do." "Now I find out we have stragglers."

"You plan on stopping us?" Thomas asked.

Azrael opened his mouth to counter, only to be interrupted by a woman's voice yelling for us to wait.

"Don't go yet," Darby insisted, appearing at Simon's bedroom door. Her pallor was no better than it had been in the moments after her body had evacuated a hundred thousand souls. Her skin was just as pale as mine, and her hair had lightened to almost white in the midst of everything. I had to wonder if she was closer to death than any of us were comfortable with. Her breaths heaved through her lungs like she'd run all the way here—which given that Bishop was nowhere to be seen—might actually have been a possibility.

"You're supposed to be resting," Axel growled, pinching his brow. "I could have sworn I told you to stay hooked up to that IV and down Dahlia's herbal remedy. Are you ignoring everything everyone is saying today, or is it just me?"

Darby shot him an irritated glare, her shoulders still heaving as she held up an intact saline bag with the tubing still attached to her hand. "I'm still hooked up, but if you think I'm letting ya'll leave without me hugging my sister—especially after she saved my fucking life—well, I can't fix that level of stupid."

She marched over to me. Well, marching was an overeager estimate for what she was doing. A wobbly hobble was closer to the mark, but she did it with gusto, so I didn't say anything to the contrary. Her hands reached for mine, squeezing my fingers as she studied my face. "You know, I thought I wouldn't miss reading everyone's thoughts, but right now, I kind of wish I still could." She opened her mouth, tears welling in her eyes. "I'm sorry you have to do this. I'm sorry you have to fight this battle for me. I'm——"

I cut her off with a hug, tempering my squeeze so I wouldn't crush her fragile body. I couldn't handle her apologizing for things that were totally out of her control. Not today and probably not any other day, either.

"I don't blame you. I wouldn't ever blame you. And, hey. Maybe I'll look in on Killian for you," I offered. "Tell him you said hi."

Darby's answering laugh quickly turned into a sob, and she returned my hug with a fierceness I hadn't expected from someone on Death's doorstep. "If you see him, can you tell him he was a wonderful dad for me? And then come back, okay? But if it's a question, I'd rather you just come back."

Swallowing the lump in my throat, I nodded into her shoulder. She pulled away, wiping at her eyes and nose. "Now get moving so you can be home before I know it or some other timey-wimey bullshit."

"What? No hug for me?" Azrael joked, staring at

my sister in a way that said his words were less a joke and more of a request.

Darby stared at him, the betrayal still radiating from every part of her. It was no secret that the pair of us blamed him for our misfortune, but she resented him far less than I did. Maybe it was because she had seen his life through his ring. Maybe she empathized better than I did.

Or maybe it was because she hadn't died yet. It was all fun and games until you got stabbed in the heart by a brother you knew nothing about.

Not that I spoke from personal experience or anything.

Instead of hugging him, Darby held out her hand to shake. Azrael stared at her hand, giving it a wry smile before taking it in both of his own. He gazed lovingly at her face for a moment, then he pulled her to him, placing a gentle kiss to her forehead.

As soon as his lips touched her skin, her whole body sagged. At first, I didn't understand, but instantly, her skin flushed with color, the gray pallor disappearing. Her hair bled of the rest of its color, changing to the same shade as mine. She wrapped her arms around his waist, squeezing him for just a moment, and then she let go.

Tears were in her eyes when she stepped back, and she gave him a silent nod before turning and leaving the room, her hasty departure sending a niggle of unease through me. Tough, since I was full to the brim with those niggles already, but she managed it.

"Time to go," Azrael muttered, his throat a little clogged.

Yep, not worried at all about what I just saw. Not even a little.

"I take it you still have the entrance path lit?" my father asked Simon.

Simon himself blushed deeply as Azrael raised a single dark eyebrow. "It's possible that the path through is lit with torches."

I narrowed my eyes at the death mage, wondering just how he knew about the whole toe thing. He pulled everything together so quickly, he had to have done it before, right?

In answer to my mental question, Simon lifted the shrunken head, an audible click reverberating through the room as a dusty bookcase swung into the space to reveal a drafty stone corridor. Torches flickered in the domed hallway, the scent of gentle decay and the musty odor of a place long-since sealed wafted into the room.

"See, no one has gone through that door in a century or more."

Simon had a door to the Underworld just chilling in

his creepy dungeon lair? Honestly, I couldn't say it was surprising. Not at all.

Azrael gave him a fatherly smile. "And the illustrious Clementine?"

Simon's lips pressed together so hard they turned white before he raised a petulant eyebrow. "There are other doors. More heavily guarded ones. Ones that eventually get you caught and locked up for decades."

The story of Clem's resurrection was starting to become clearer in my mind.

"I see. Do take care to guard it after us, will you?" I supposed that was Azrael-speak for "Essex was on his way here, so maybe don't open it for the nefarious bastard, mm-kay?"

My father gave me an indulgent smile and nodded to the open door. "Time to go," he repeated, only this time he wasn't about to start bawling. I considered this a good sign.

Bastian crossed the room and hugged his brother, slapping his back hard enough to rattle Simon's teeth before he came back to me and grabbed my hand. We then followed Azrael as he led us through the door, the chill making me shiver as our steps echoed through the hallway. Thomas and Axel trailed after us, their footfalls adding to the quiet cacophony that was our trek to the Underworld.

No one said anything for a long while, the echoes of our footfalls creating a gentle rhythm that was slightly unnerving. This little hallway seemed no different than Simon's dungeon, the cool, dry air less telling than it should have been. I mean, this was the Underworld. Shouldn't there be like a flashing neon sign, or a black hole or something that said, "Hey, you're dead" around here somewhere? I wasn't asking for something off the Vegas Strip, but a teensy feeling in my gut would have done the trick.

That didn't come until much later.

The only clue I got that something was amiss was when Axel and Thomas' steps faltered. Or rather, when those faltering steps turned into Thomas collapsing in the middle of the corridor and Axel growling at him to stay the fuck down.

"I'm fine," Thomas said tersely, pushing himself to standing with the liberal help of the stone wall. Granted, his legs gave out within a few seconds, but it was the macho principle of the thing, right?

Axel stood tall, staring at Thomas like he'd lost his mind. "Yeah, and I'm the Easter bunny. You've been stumbling for ten minutes, you idiot. I think when you shrivel to dust, they're gonna notice."

"I'm *fine*," Thomas repeated before a cough racked his whole body. Dutifully, he covered his mouth, only for his fingers to come away coated in red. "I just need a minute."

Azrael crowded the men, kneeling to assess Thomas in that unnerving way of his. "Would you have my daughter blame herself for your death?"

He'd asked the same thing of Bishop only an hour ago, and like Bishop, Thomas looked like he'd just swallowed bile.

He wasn't the only one. I'd promised to protect Thomas—and he, me—once upon a time. I wasn't sure I could live with myself if he died trying to pay me back for something I was going to do anyway.

Sighing, he answered, "Of course not."

Azrael raised an imperious eyebrow. "Then get your head out of your ass and allow your friend to take you back to the door. Beings like you are too old, too powerful to be masked by a little death. You knew this when you walked in here. I commend your bravery. Your stupidity, however, is going to get you into trouble one of these days." He hauled Thomas to his feet so the vampire could throw an arm over Axel's shoulder.

"Run. Fast."

Both Thomas and Axel gave me a rueful look, and then they were gone, Axel hefting the vamp over his shoulder as he took off.

I watched them go far longer than I should have, and Bastian stayed with me, our eyes on the corridor until we couldn't see them anymore.

14

We walked for ages.

We walked so much, I could have sworn we had been in this corridor for days, weeks even. When we came to a door—as glorious a sight as that was—Azrael opened it without a second's hesitation.

I, however, needed a bit of coaxing.

It didn't matter that this was a way out of the dumbest, longest, most boring hallway known to the universe, walking into the actual Underworld didn't sound like a vacation to me. And no, it didn't matter that the place looked like a carbon copy of a suburb circa 1965. In fact, that was the supreme reason I didn't want to step one toe—pun totally intended—over the threshold.

Azrael was not down with my foolishness and latched onto my hand, yanking me—and by default, Bastian—into the creepiest little neighborhood I'd ever seen. Maybe it was because I'd watched one too many horror movies, but a completely deserted subdivision pinged my not-okay radar. Hell, I'd take the dirty streets of Ascension over the too-manicured lawns and sweet daisy wind chimes.

Hard pass.

Add in the too-bright sky with no visible sun and no way to see the horizon, complete lack of a breeze and... Not just no, but *hell* no.

"It's just Purgatory. Get a grip," Azrael grumbled, pulling me by the hand as my reluctant feet slowed us down.

"Purgatory a la *Supernatural* or *The Good Place*, because those are two very different things from two very different shows, and—"

Azrael stared at me like I had a recently formed hole in the middle of my forehead. "I've been locked in a prison for twenty years, Sloane. Under rocks and dirt and an entire lake. Cut me some slack and elaborate."

I dithered—actually dithered—waffling my hand from side to side. "Well, *Supernatural* would mean that all the monsters are sent here when they die, and we have to fight them to stay alive zombie-apocalypse style.

The Good Place would mean that things are mildly inconvenient, and we have to become better people to ascend to the actual good place."

Bastian snorted out a laugh from behind his fist, while Azrael continued to stare at me like I was an alien.

"What? I didn't have much of a social life when I was alive. TV shows were my jam. At least I didn't bring up *The Vampire Diaries* or *Wynona Earp*. Their versions just don't seem as plausible."

Azrael just shook his head and turned, marching down the middle of a street that could have been copied straight out of *Pleasantville*. Grumbling, I stomped after him, wondering why there couldn't have been a speedier way to get where we needed to go. Wasn't he the Angel of Death? Didn't he do this shit in his sleep?

"Just because I am who I am doesn't mean I run things down here," he grumbled, shaking his head as he answered my unasked question. "Truth be told, I'm more like a messenger or a bus driver. People up there fear me because I'm the first person they see after what is likely the worst day of their existence. Humans and the arcane alike fear me because I seem so final. Arcaners try to extend their lives, try to stay on that little rock as long as they possibly can. Little do they know there is so much more. Take your friend Thomas for example. He's been alive since the Qin Dynasty, and still, he fears me. Over two thousand years on the planet, and he still worries what will happen when he dies."

Ho-ly shit. Thomas was that old? I had an inkling he was older than dirt, but I didn't know he was BC-era old.

"And you think just because I play ferryman, I have any control whatsoever down here?" He shook his head again, still marching. "I control fuck all."

Out of the corner of my eye, I thought I caught a glimpse of blonde hair, but as soon as I turned my head, it was gone. One of those mid-century modern daisy wind chimes with the too-happy faces and unbearably loud colors was moving, even though I couldn't feel a breeze.

Sure. Nothing to see here.

Bastian frowned, mouthing a "You okay?" at me, but I shook my head. This was one of those times where I wished I could speak inside his head like he sometimes did to me. Though, I was pretty sure that was a remnant of dear old dad's powers if I was being honest.

"Okay, so we have to take the scenic route," I replied, trying not to freak out. "Care to share how long you think that will be, or how the hell we get out of here?"

He shrugged, still stomping toward who knew where in this creepy-as-fuck neighborhood. And the creep factor went up to a thousand the first time I heard the giggle. It was cheery and feminine, and exactly what I did not want to hear in the middle of a deserted Purgatory with Grumpy McGrouch as my tour guide.

Honestly, I wanted a bazooka or some napalm or something, because I figured any minute a giant sand-worm was going to bust out of the ground and eat me whole.

"Sandworms? And what the hell is *Beetlejuice?*" Azrael griped, shaking his head *again* as we came to a street sign. A completely useless street sign to be clear.

The street we were on? Purgatory Lane.

The cross street? Purgatory Avenue.

"It's not like you've been reassuring me that we aren't going to get stabbed to not-death in the middle of this creepy neighborhood that seems to have no end. What the hell am I supposed to think when wind chimes start moving on their own and I hear disem-bodied giggles? That things are going to turn up tea and roses? Let's not forget that I'm only here in the first place because of you!" At this point, I was jabbing my finger into a death deity's chest as I stared at him right in the eyes.

I was floating. Again.

Then those giggles sounded again—a fuck of a lot closer this time—and my feet found the pavement all on their own.

Azrael's eyes widened as he stared just past me, the giggles turning softer as they got closer.

"It's right behind me, isn't it?"

Bastian and I froze—or rather, I froze, and Bastian whipped around, pulling me behind his back as he faced whatever it was. Instead of a sandworm or a monster wielding a machete, there stood a blonde woman with flowers weaved through her curls and a serene expression on her practically cherubic face. But her features wavered like mine sometimes did, turning from a pretty blonde hippy to a severe raven-haired woman.

She assessed the three of us with her exacting gaze, her form flickering back and forth between the happy blonde and angry brunette, only... the longer she flickered, the more the features seemed to settle until she turned into a strange mixture of both.

Bastian shuffled us back, doing his best to keep himself between the woman and me. Given that he was the only non-dead one of us, I figured this was probably a horrible idea on his part. But the woman simply smiled through her assessment, staring at Bastian as if he was simply adorable and she wanted to pinch his cheeks or something.

"My, aren't you precious?" she cooed, breaking out into a bout of giggles that equally filled my heart with joy and creeped me all the way out. "You remind me of my husband in that way. But you're not supposed to be here. I don't care what you try to use to disguise yourself. Your time is not quite up." She peeked around Bastian to peer at me. "And you, my dear, should have been here ages ago. I take it it's his fault?" She lifted her chin at Azrael before sticking out her tongue at him. "Is there anyone you haven't brought back yet?"

Azrael huffed out a withering chuckle. "Essex?"

The woman rolled her eyes. "Of all your children that you have brought to me, why haven't you hauled that dumbass down here yet?"

"The ru—"

She waved her hand at him dismissively. "Yes, yes. The *rules*. You know, you're the only one who follows them anymore. And if there were anyone to break your rules for, it's that miscreant." Her gaze flickered back to me. "I'm Persephone, by the way. It's very nice to meet you, Sloane. I've heard a lot about you. Not from this one," she grumbled, casting her gaze from Azrael back to me, "but your parents. They really are lovely people."

She could have bowled me over with a feather, but she chose a brick instead.

"You've met them?" I whispered, my eyes welling.

What is with them leaking all the damn time?

There were other questions I had, too, but they were ones I couldn't ask. Not with what I was now. My mother and father and hell, even Otis wouldn't recognize me now. I might have done some good, might have saved some people, but in their eyes, I'd be a monster.

I was sure of it.

"Of course I've met them. I greet all the new residents of Elysium personally. Azrael escorted them directly. They didn't even have to wait in line."

Don't know where you're going, huh? No shortcuts, huh? What a crock of shit.

"Are they…" I couldn't even finish that question.

Are they okay? Do they know what I am now? Do they hate me? Can I see them? Are they safe? Is Otis okay?

Bastian wrapped an arm around my shoulder and pressed a kiss to my forehead. Maybe it was because I was shaking. Maybe it was because I was holding in my sobs with the efficiency of a toddler who'd just gotten their first spanking. Or maybe he knew just how bad all this hurt, how much I missed them, how much I hoped they didn't hate what I'd become.

"They're wonderful. They look in on you from time to time. Your mother is so proud of you. You know, she was quite the blood mage in her prime. Fought in the 1812 Blood Wars to boot. She sent many people our way over the years—just like you."

I wanted to feel relief—I really did. But it just didn't come.

"Since you're here, would you like to meet my family?" she asked, her odd eyes flashing back and forth from a lush grass green to a purple so dark it might as well have been black.

Did I? Honestly, the answer was a solid "Not particularly," but I had a feeling if I said so it would offend her. That fact was no more evident when Azrael prodded me in the ribs.

Oh, right. They can read my thoughts. Way to go, Sloane.

"Sure," I said, my voice a solid monotone. "I'd love to meet the family. It sounds like fun."

Persephone snickered. "I like her. I get why you brought her back. Way better choice than that dunderhead you call a son. Tell me again why you've let him live so long?"

"You know I don't break the ru—"

"Rules," she said, rolling her eyes. "Yes, yes. I remember. Okay, everyone, follow me."

Persephone led us to one of the creepy too-perfect houses, the manicured lawn and exactly perfect driveway a testament to the fact that no one lived here. I'd had a good home in a nice neighborhood. The houses were well-kept, and the lawns mowed. But there were imperfections, too—that's what made them perfect. There was the errant weed or bike not put away. There was sidewalk-chalked driveways and toys left out. And the sounds. The memory of those sounds called to my soul. Dogs barking, lawn mowers humming, people talking about nothing. It was a soundtrack of a wonderful childhood.

And even though it had been a lie, I still cherished it. Maybe that made me stupid, but I didn't care.

This neighborhood was scary to me because of its ordered perfection, and I figured that was the point.

Persephone opened the front door to reveal an elevator, the large cubicle big enough to fit us all and then some. It was one of those super-fancy elevators that required a key. She pulled a golden one out of her pocket, stuck it in the slot, and pressed the button for the penthouse.

Yeah, and that wasn't terrifying or anything.

15

In the back of my mind, I knew I was meeting Hades, sure, but the reality of it was a sight more surreal than anything I'd anticipated. It was one thing to binge Hades and Persephone romance novels as a young teen and quite another to be meeting them in the actual flesh.

The elevator ride was mostly silent and awkward, with Azrael looking like he was being taken to the gallows, and Bastian and I trying not to hysterically giggle at the highly inappropriate time. We were taking an elevator to go meet the King of the Underworld for fuck's sake. Not only did that not make any sense at all, but I was also running on the assumption that we most definitely were not supposed to be here.

Hell, if Azrael's face was anything to go by, we were

about to be screwed seven ways to Sunday. And not in a good way.

The elevator dinged, the little "PH" on the floor indicator lighting up before the doors opened. Persephone breezed through them with no question in her mind that we'd follow her. Truth be told, we didn't have any other choice. It was either meet whomever she wanted us to or go back downstairs to the neighborhood that never ended.

At least if Hades smited me, I wouldn't have to traipse through there anymore. *Is it smited? Smote? What is the correct term for getting blown to smithereens by the King of the Underworld?*

We emerged from the elevator before Persephone flitted out of sight, following the sound of a dog whine and the tell-tale sound of happy puppy nails on tile. Everything about the penthouse felt like money. Like all the money in the universe was used to build this place. The floors were the whitest of marble, veined with what had to be pure gold. The walls were papered in rich linen with the faintest hint of a shimmer to them. Sconces dotted the entrance, the light from them pure magic.

I'd felt like I shouldn't have been here *before* I witnessed this level of luxury, and now that I had, I had the distinct feeling that I was somehow dirty. My hands were clean, and I had no visible signs of walking for what felt like days, but me in combat leathers and shit-kickers absolutely did not belong here. I met Bastian's gaze, and it seemed he, too, felt distinctly like Pig Pen from *Peanuts*, complete with that miasma of dirt following our every move.

Reluctantly rounding the corner, we caught sight of the goddess curled around a giant of a dog, its three heads trying to lick her face as she giggled.

"Honestly," she said, mock-scolding the hound, "I was only gone for a few minutes."

"A few minutes too long," a man said, striding into the room, his deep voice practically reverberating through my skull.

If Azrael was tall, this man was an actual giant, and formidable didn't even begin to cover it. The first thing I noticed about him—after the height, of course—were the scars that crisscrossed his cheeks, running down his jaw and into the collar of his shirt. The second was the impossible darkness in his eyes. I'd thought I'd seen black before, but this was something else. His hair was white like mine, which offset his dark skin like stars in the sky, the strands falling over his shoulders and down his back. He was beautiful and terrifying just like his wife.

And I could only assume this was Hades. Mostly

because it seemed to take him a long while to notice us, his focus taken by the woman cuddling the three-headed dog. I'd always wondered if the famed Cerberus was actually three dogs in one body or a collective mind with three heads. It had bothered me to no end when I'd studied Greek mythology, though the mythology part seemed less and less of a myth nowadays.

"A bit of both, actually," the man rumbled, meeting my gaze with his pitch-black stare. His accent wasn't quite British nor was it American. It wasn't thick or hard to understand, but it held a gravity that spoke of several millennia of languages amalgamated into a singular dialect.

I jolted when he answered my question, which made him smile at me like I was adorable.

"You were wondering if Cerberus was three dogs or one. He's both."

Well, that clears everything right up.

Hades huffed at my internal cheek, giving me a wry smile. "He has three minds, but they run on a collective knowledge. Each head feels different emotions, sees different things, but all the information is shared, so he's both."

That actually did clear everything up.

"Glad I could help. Seph, what have you brought

me?" he asked, crossing his arms over his enormous chest.

Persephone gave Cerberus another pat on each head before straightening to look at our unruly little trio. "A wayward god with some serious familial issues, his daughter, and her not even remotely dead lover."

Hades frowned, not bothering to stare at anyone but me, which was super unnerving and not a little scary. "And she had hundreds of thousands of souls stuck inside her because?"

"Yeah, *Dad*, share with the class," I asked, whipping my head to the side to spear Azrael with my death glare. "Why do I have an inordinate number of souls just chilling inside my body?"

Azrael sighed as he pinched his brow.

Hades chuckled. "Wait, don't tell me. Essex, right? Please tell me again why you haven't reduced him to ash by now. You know none of us would think less of you. Even me."

Considering Hades had been literally eaten by his father, that was a pretty bold statement. Though, it was a complete mystery why Azrael hadn't killed Essex by now. It wasn't like he didn't have the means.

"You know why," Azrael answered. "The ru—"

"Rules." Hades cut him off. "Yes, I remember your faithfulness to those silly things. Don't you know by now that some rules were meant to be broken?" Hades paused, assessing me. "Though, your penchant for bringing people back from the dead does get tiring. Luckily, your daughter has sent us plenty of souls to make up for it."

"I brought one person back. One. *She* brought *him* back. That one is not my fault."

Hades blinked at him, his white eyebrow lifting in a way that was both comical and terrifying. "And what do death mages do again? Who do they make deals with for resurrections? I can't remember."

Azrael let out an irritated sigh. "Those are one-for-one trades. Those don't count, and you know it."

"Whatever you say." Hades gestured down the corridor. "Please come in. My home is your home. Would you like some food?"

Without waiting for an acceptance, Hades turned, walking hand in hand with his wife as they led us toward a mammoth dining table set for six. Already seated was a woman with a big black dog resting its head in her lap. Every few seconds she would tear pieces of meat from the drumstick on her plate and feed it to the beautiful animal.

Persephone motioned to one of the open seats. "Sit. Eat. You all must be tired after that trek."

Etiquette had never been my strong suit, but when

it came to being offered food from gods, I couldn't tell if accepting would have me turned into a monster or not.

Before I could rein in my mouth, I asked, "This isn't like the Fae realm, right? Eating offered food isn't going to make it so I can't ever leave or something?"

Bastian elbowed me in the arm, but I just shrugged at him.

Excuse the hell out of me for being the smart one here.

The woman with the dog started laughing, wiping tears from her odd, blue-tinged skin. Her hair was black, pin-straight, and adorned with tiny, jeweled keys. In her ears were these strikingly beautiful gold earrings that looked like twined snakes.

Big black dog, snakes, and keys? I was putting money on this being Hecate.

"You'd be right." She smiled at me and also gestured for me to sit down. "Come eat. No one plans on making you a prisoner, and the fruit salad is quite delicious."

Awkwardly, I sat across from the woman as she inspected Bastian. He sat at my left with far more grace than I had, placing his napkin on his lap and keeping his mouth shut. Beside him was Persephone who gleefully passed him a large bowl of fruit with candied nuts and what smelled of a coconut and lime sauce. Hades passed me a platter filled with a gloriously fragrant meat. It looked like turkey legs—like the ones you'd get at a fair—only this was so much better. I passed Bastian the platter as Hecate handed over a basket of bread.

Soon, we were all eating. Hades, Persephone, and Hecate ribbed Azrael good-naturedly, but all the while, he seemed more and more uncomfortable—as if he'd rather be anywhere but here. He picked at his food, feeding most of it to the dog at Hecate's side. When he got quieter and quieter, Hecate engaged Bastian in a rousing debate over the merits of totems in casting work—a subject I found fascinating but still had no idea what they were talking about. As my plate emptied, Hades quietly got my attention. And by quietly, I meant he spoke inside my head.

You and I need to have a chat. Come to the balcony for a drink.

It was unnerving when Bastian's thoughts resounded in my skull, but Hades was a whole other animal. I was pretty sure my teeth rattled. There was no other choice, really. I got up, pressed a kiss to Bastian's cheek, and followed Hades out a set of glass doors that led to a giant balcony.

It was no secret I was afraid of heights, so when I stepped outside, I stuck close to the wall and kept my eyes on my feet. We were in that elevator for what felt like forever. There was no way I was going to look down from this height.

No way, no how.

"How can a dead woman be afraid of heights?" Hades asked as he mixed a cocktail at an ornate bar cart next to a pair of teak patio chairs. In a few moments his ministrations produced what appeared to be a mojito, the mint plucked fresh from a lush potted plant. He offered me a glass and I sipped dutifully, thinking of a good answer.

"Have you ever tried to…" I began, still trying to think of a way to explain.

"To end it? No, I can't say I have. But I get your point. You associate heights with pain and therefore you fear them."

When he put it like that, it made me feel sort of stupid. I was already dead, so death was sort of off the table. Plus, I was in the Underworld. I literally could not get deader if I tried. I took a hesitant step toward the stone railing, looking out on the world below. Banding the building in a lush mote was a dense forest dotted with ancient ruins, their jagged spines reaching for the sky. Past that was a river that had several forks, each one leading in a different direction.

"I wonder what you'll do when you get your wings."

I nearly choked on an ice cube and had to pound on my chest to get the damn thing to go down. "What? Wings?"

Hades smiled at me bemusedly. "You'll take over for Azrael, right? That job comes with wings, you know."

Taking over for Azrael? "Sure. Maybe in a thousand years or so I'll get used to the idea of flying around on wings. For now, though, the thought of flying anywhere—*ever*—sounds like a horrible idea."

"I see. Do you understand what he does?"

I waffled my hand. "In theory. I've read the mythologies. Doesn't mean that's the truth, though, does it? The Greeks never liked the thought of a peaceful death."

"None of the living like death much. They fear it and paint it as the end, but it never has been. There are those—even his own children—that see what he does and hate him for it, begging for more time when all your father is, is an instrument of Fate. But he never gained balance. Never thought to carve out happiness for himself. When I was younger, I made the same mistakes. Until I found Seph, that is."

He sipped his drink in silence, letting me digest what a lonely existence Azrael had had. It made me sad for him, made me curse Essex for enacting a revenge that had never been fair.

"I want you to have balance and rest. The dead aren't going anywhere. When it's your time to follow in Azrael's footsteps, I want you to realize that balance, that love will see you through on your darkest days."

He was talking like I would be taking the job now. "I've got time, though, right? You're talking like this is happening tomorrow."

Hades gave me an enigmatic smile. "Not tomorrow."

Well, that wasn't cryptic at all.

"Since I've got you here, you know a way to get these souls out of me so I don't have to continue traipsing through the Underworld like a newbie?" I paused, deciding whether or not I wanted to ask this next bit. "And maybe go visit a few of your residents?"

Originally, I'd planned on trying to swing by to make sure Killian was where Azrael said he was after I was purged, but now that I knew that Persephone had seen my parents with her own eyes, well… It was probably a pipe dream, anyway.

"I *could* take those souls out of you right now, but then you would need to go home. If you were to travel to Elysium and send them to their rest yourself, you could possibly visit a few of the residents there. Plus, I figure if I give you an incentive, you might actually learn something about this place."

There was only one problem. Bastian was alive. Sure, he'd died once before, but it wasn't his time— Persephone had said so herself. What if it took too long? What if Essex attacked while we were gone? What if Bastian never made it out of here? What if Thomas and Axel never made it to the door?

What if…

"What if you worry about those things once you can actually do something about them? Go to Elysium, kid. You're too young to be worried about so much." Then he stood, offering me his mitt of a hand to shake. I took it without hesitation. "I look forward to working with you soon, Sloane."

"Not that soon," I quipped.

I hoped I wasn't lying.

16

Eventually, Bastian came to collect me, breaking my reverie of the vast and obscenely beautiful land below. I could almost see Elysium. The path wasn't exactly easy, but this bird's eye view at the very least gave us a heading. What I wouldn't give for a compass or a map or even a reliable tour guide.

I was staring at the broken spires snaking their way up through the trees when I felt a welcome kiss on my neck. At some point, Hades had left me to my ponderings, and now Bastian was here kissing my neck as I gazed upon a beautiful but a little terrifying landscape.

"You ready to go, love?" he murmured, wrapping an arm around my middle.

Was I ready to go? I wasn't so sure.

"Would it be so bad to stay here? To live here?" The question was out of my mouth before I really thought it through. I could do this—balance my love for Bastian while holding a job that was necessary and vital. We could live here, make a home where my awful brother couldn't attack us. Absorb the beauty of a place like this and just be. It wasn't a fully formed idea, and I had not a single clue about whether it would work or not, but Hades had planted the seed in my mind.

"I think if we could come and go as we pleased, it wouldn't be so bad. But I think if we couldn't, we would miss everyone, don't you?"

He was right, and it hurt. It hurt for so many reasons, but the number one was that I knew it would make every single person we loved regret letting us go. Turning in his arms, I fit my nose into the crook of his shoulder.

"I don't want to leave them behind, either," I admitted, leaving off the fact that I felt almost at peace here, felt almost home. But the Night Watch was my home, too.

Bastian was my home. And Thomas and Clem and Simon and Dahlia. Axel and Emrys and Darby. Harper. Ingrid. Hell, I was even almost warming up to Bishop—even though I still thought he wasn't good enough for my sister.

If I could avoid leaving them behind, I would.

"I have a choice to make," I murmured into his skin, not wanting to look at his face as I told him my selfish plan. "I can let Hades remove the souls trapped inside me, set them free in an instant, and the three of us would immediately go back home. *Or* we can traverse the Underworld and take them to Elysium where they are meant to be."

Bastian pushed me back, his bottle-green eyes staring right down to my soul. "And by going to Elysium, it means you could maybe see your parents, talk to Darby's dad, give him her last goodbye."

It had to be a joint decision. I couldn't make it on my own with no one's input. That just wasn't fair. "Yes, that's about the gist of it."

"Do you honestly think I could say no to you?"

I shoved at his shoulder a little, jostling him. "But it's not just me here. It's all of us."

He reeled me in, pulling me tight to his chest as he pressed a kiss to my temple. His fingers toyed with my braid as he shook his head. "If it were me wanting to see my parents, what would you do?"

I did not like that he was this insightful.

"You would snatch me by the hand and march to the doors, hammering at them until Hades himself let you in. You would scour the whole of this realm just to make me happy. Don't act like you wouldn't make the same sacrifices for me as I would for you, love."

It really was annoying when he was this damn perfect. "Are you sure?"

He raised an imperious eyebrow at me.

"Fine," I muttered, pressing a kiss to his lips. "You're sure."

When it was time to leave, Persephone directed us to a different elevator, her trusty three-headed dog at her side. She rubbed at the fur on the center head as she pressed the ornate call button.

"If you get a chance, come back and see me," she instructed. "I'd love to talk a bit more, get to know you. Plus, it's so refreshing to see a new face around here."

Smiling, I said, "Of course. We'll come back around this way on our way out."

Her smile was genuine, but it had a tinge of something more, something bittersweet. Then the elevator dinged, and we piled on without her.

"I'll see you soon," she said, the statement far more ominous than intended, and the door closed, cutting us off from the pretty penthouse and thrusting us downward.

Far faster than my stomach would have liked, we

reached the ground floor, the mechanical ding of the elevator announcing our arrival. The doors opened to reveal a lush forest, the likes of which I glimpsed from the top floor. I'd assumed the trees were dense, but I had no idea that the place was out of a Grimm fairytale.

The trees twisted and turned, their trunks crooked and jagged as if someone had constructed them from a fever dream. The imperceptible sun seemed unable to reach us under the canopy, the darkness a touch too ominous for me.

"This is creepier than the suburb, for sure," Bastian said, but Azrael and I scoffed at him.

"No way. Maybe you haven't seen enough horror movies, but that 'hood was about a millisecond from being a *Hitchcock* movie," I countered, an involuntary shudder quaking through my body as I walked.

Azrael had the good sense to nod. "A whole world full of nothing or a dark forest. I'll take the forest, thank you."

I bumped Azrael's shoulder with mine—or rather, I bumped his elbow with my shoulder, but whatever. "Good man. It's always important to side with the daughter in these types of situations. We're always right."

"I'll remember that." He paused, staring at his

shoes before speaking again. "Did you have a good talk with Hades?"

I shrugged, kicking a rock as I went. "It was a little bittersweet and a lot confusing, but I couldn't say it was the worst thing I've done today. You didn't seem like you were comfortable there. I thought these people were your family?"

He grumbled intelligibly. "They are, and they aren't. We've known each other so long, it seems like it sometimes. But they're different from me. They see the aftermath of what I do, and..." He stuffed his hands in his pockets. "They are fulfilled here in a way I have never been. They have made this place their home, and I have always been on this outside with one foot in both worlds."

I bumped him again. "Maybe you could find a nice lady and settle down. One you hopefully don't impregnate immediately and actually get to know. That could be nice, right?"

He rolled his eyes at my jab. "I knew them all before I—never mind."

Snorting, I skipped ahead and began walking backward so I could taunt him. "Had s-e-x with them?" I whispered behind my hand. "Does that help your delicate sensibilities?"

He lifted his face skyward, probably asking whichever god that controlled patience to throw him a bone. "Why don't you ask the question you really want to ask? Did I love your mother?"

That had my feet stalling. It had been a question that had flitted through my mind, but one I didn't give much thought to. Or at least I thought I hadn't. Until that very second, I hadn't realized just how important his answer was or why I needed to know.

"Did you?"

A soft smile graced his lips before he stared right into my eyes. "Yes. I loved your mother as much as I was able. She brought me so much peace when I was with her that I wanted to stay, but..." He shook his head. "I wasn't what she needed. Rosalind needed someone stronger, someone who would stick around for the hard stuff. As much as I loved her, I—I couldn't be there. Not all the time. And it wasn't just the job that kept me away. Being around the living is hard for someone like me."

A sadness hunched his shoulders as he kicked a rock on the trail. "We ended it when she got pregnant with you. She said that the love of her life was in her belly, and she wasn't going to let her settle for scraps as she had. At the time, I'd thought I'd been a good partner, but I realized then that I would let you down. Peter came into her life when she was four months along and was there in every single way I couldn't have been. Loved her in all the ways I couldn't. And in the end, he died trying to protect you from my mistake. They both did."

Pivoting on a foot, I stalked farther into the trees, trying to keep sight of the path in the gloom. I'd been kidding. Why did he have to go and make me feel sorry for him, huh? I'd been just fine hating him this whole time. Why did he have to make me see myself in him?

Because that was the kicker, wasn't it? Azrael saw himself as other, as different, as a monster. When it came to stepping up and staying, he left because he thought it was better for everyone else.

I wonder where I've heard that before.

"I guess you got more from me than just hair color."

I snorted. "Yeah, a brother from Hell *and* generational trauma. Thanks a bunch, *Dad*."

He began moving again, bumping me with his hip as he passed. "What can I say? I'm a giver like that."

At least I know where I got my sarcasm from.

He let out a gleeful laugh. "Oh, no. That was a gift bestowed upon you from both sides. Your mother"— He shook his head—"she was the reigning queen of sarcasm. Do you know how we met?"

Obviously, I didn't. Mom hadn't spoken one word about him my whole life.

"It was on the battlefield. She had just ripped through an entire battalion with a blood-boiling curse —just popping people's brains like balloons. Given what it is I do, I was there to reap the souls. Even under cover of night and my natural glamour, she still saw me. Even tried killing me, too, until she figured out who I was."

He stared off in the distance at the memory, a fondness taking over his whole face. "She was magnificent. Had a tongue just as sharp as her spells. And the fire she had, the fierceness with which she protected you..."

It was tough to see my mother through this lens— the battle-hungry and bloodthirsty mage—when all I had known of her was the mom who complained about charcoal stains on my white sheets. He knew her in a way I never could, and I wished that I could have grown up just catching a glimpse of the woman he described. Still, I missed the mother I had. The one who giggled with me about high school shenanigans, the one who patched up bloody knees and gave me the best hugs.

The one who did everything she could for me, all the time. Even if I hadn't met the warrior, I still got the best mom. The very best one.

"She was a good mom," I croaked, and if tears raced down my cheeks, well, then that was allowed.

"Yes. She was. And she chose a fabulous partner to raise you. I will be forever grateful for that."

Swallowing hard, I forced my feet forward. "He was a good dad."

For some reason thinking about Dad hurt a lot. Maybe it was because he hadn't known what he was getting into with me and Mom.

"Yes, he did," Azrael countered, dashing that misconception as fast as it slipped through my thoughts. "He knew from the start. Your mom made sure of it. Peter was with her every step of the way, through everything. They didn't have any secrets—not even about you."

I couldn't say why that filled me with a sense of relief. Maybe it was because it felt less like an unwanted betrayal on my part—that he'd died in my defense and didn't know why. But he knew.

He knew and he'd stayed.

For me.

For us.

Bastian startled me when he grabbed my hand, pulling me to a stop so hard, I nearly fell. Then I heard it—the rustling in the trees. The branches creaked as if something heavy were resting on them, and that filled me with an inordinate amount of dread.

Stupidly, I looked up, meeting the golden eyes of a bird. Or, maybe not. Owl-like eyes blinked at me from a distinctly feminine face that was a startling mix of both woman and bird, her sharp beak hooked and lethal. Her dark hair hung in a rope down over her shoulder, mixing liberally with her feathers, and instead of arms, she had wings.

My brain supplied the species: *Harpy.*

And she wasn't alone.

Oh, no, this bird lady had friends. A whole fucking flock filled the trees above our heads, their feathers ruffling as they stared menacingly down on us.

We were officially in deep, deep shit.

17

I'd sort of figured my luck was bad, but a whole flock of harpies just lying in wait to murder me? That was next-level bad luck of epic proportions. Honestly, it wasn't even fair.

I didn't know if it was because I'd looked up or the fact that Azrael took that moment to make a noise, but at the sound, the whole fucking group decided it was high time they took the plunge—each one sailing off their perches to dive bomb us. The collective screech was enough to make my ears bleed.

Without so much as a nod toward decorum— because let's face it, harpies were completely out of our wheelhouse—Bastian and I took off running.

Here's the thing they don't tell you about harpies in school—

yes, I know they don't cover magical beings in Biology, just go with it—they are fast.

Like really fast.

Like could flip off a Peregrine falcon while in their sleep as they zoomed past it yawning, fast.

So, it didn't matter that I was a little more juiced up than usual—not that the effects of having that many souls just chilling under my flesh had given me so much as a blip of the problems Darby had—I wasn't getting away from these ladies without some serious injuries. Also, fun fact about the Underworld? Bastian's fun ability to slow time didn't work here.

Trust me, he tried it.

Bastian grabbed me by my arm, whipping me around so I was curled over his shoulders, and then we went exactly nowhere. There was no dip in my belly or slew of trees speeding past us. We weren't that lucky, but considering I'd already figured my luck was shit, it didn't exactly surprise me. Plus, being thrown over his shoulder did give me a very up close and personal look at what a harpy looked like when she went in for the kill.

Wings spread wide, she used them to slow herself, reaching her taloned feet toward my face with the expert skill of a practiced killing machine. The best I could do—and yes, I knew that my best in this situation was fucking suspect—was to knee Bastian in the chest. He stumbled, dropping us both to the ground in a bruising roll.

It hurt.

A lot.

But it did have the intended outcome of me not getting a face full of harpy claw, so at least there was that.

"Azrael," I screamed, shoving myself to my feet and yanking Bastian up with me.

But I didn't have the time to look for him—not when I heard the deafening screech of another bird lady. She was close—too close for my liking—and I latched onto Bastian, rushing through the twisted trees in a zigzag while trying not to die.

Yes, I know. I'm already dead. But whatever. Semantics. Regrowing shit fucking hurts.

Ahead looked like one of those ruins I'd spied from Hades' balcony, and I sprinted for it, hoping the cover would serve us. We were ten long steps from the stone façade when the blistering heat of agony ripped into my back. No, not just ripped.

Tore.

Gouged.

Every horrific word there was in creation couldn't possibly describe the feeling of a harpy's talons burrowed into your flesh. Then I was lifted off my feet by that dreadful *fucking* foot, hanging by my right shoulder as she attempted to carry me off.

I'd never in my life been so happy to be left-handed. Without much planning on my part, I latched onto the long dagger at my thigh and slashed up blindly.

Also, a good thing to know about harpies? They didn't waste time in the trees once their prey was acquired, nor did they keep going after prey once said prey started fighting back.

Want to know how I know?

Because as soon as I slashed, I miraculously managed to hit my target, and she dropped my ass like a hot potato. Truth be told, falling hurt a fuck of a lot less than I'd remembered. Maybe it was the sharp tree branches and twig and leaves that broke my fall, but at least I didn't go splat on the forest floor. I did manage to break an arm, cut myself on my own dagger, and take a branch upside the head, though, so that was fun.

I laid there for several seconds, waiting for the breath to come back to my lungs as I stared at the Sloane-sized hole in the canopy. Harpies raced through the air overhead, peeling off at their sister's pained cry. So, those bitches were bullies then—cutting and running as soon as someone fought back.

I'd have to remember that.

Groaning, I peeled myself up off the ground, managing to sit up without yelping in pain. Just fuck harpies and forests and the whole of the Underworld.

"Sloane," Bastian yelled, the sound reaching my ears from a decent distance. His voice was hoarse, like he'd been calling my name for quite a while.

"Here," I croaked back, my voice not even remotely loud enough. I cleared my throat and shouted louder, hoping he heard. At my shout, my whole right side took the opportunity to do a little shouting of its own, the pain radiating through me hard enough to make me gag.

Yep, in my initial assessment of my injuries, I'd missed the two broken ribs. *Good times.*

And where the fuck was Azrael? Wasn't he sort of a bigwig around here? Couldn't he have just snapped his fingers and got them to quit their bullshit?

Bastian reached me before I got the gumption to stand, the sight of his slightly bloody but otherwise unharmed self the most welcomed thing I'd seen in a hot minute.

"Jesus, fuck, Sloane," he muttered, dropping a marginally painful kiss to my forehead. "I thought... I don't know what I thought. She just snatched you right up and I..."

"I'm okay." I most certainly was *not*. "I'm alive." Again, debatable. "We're together now." Accurate.

"Where are you hurt? Do you need blood?"

The answers to that were: everywhere and yes. But drinking from him wasn't a good idea right now, especially if those harpies decided to sack up and return. He needed to be able to run, and although I didn't think me taking a few sips would be a detriment to his health, I sure as shit didn't want to risk it. Especially not here.

"I'm fine."

He huffed at me, clucking his tongue like I was an impudent child. "I have eyes, Sloane. I can see the bloody bone sticking out of your arm."

Yeah, I'd been trying really hard not to think about that.

"Let me give you a few sips of blood. We don't have time for me to carry you all over this blasted place."

"But—"

He grabbed my face gently, forcing me to meet his gaze, but his tone was the most commanding thing I had ever heard in my life. "But nothing. Drink."

At the order, my fangs began to ache, the need to feed so necessary I nearly passed out at the scent of him. It was all around me, filling my nostrils of woodsmoke and spent magic, spices and Bastian. My mouth practically started watering, and when he positioned his neck so it brushed my lips, I was done for.

I struck, my fangs piercing his flesh with the most seductive pop. Images hit me instantly, flashing one after the other in a reel of what could be. Things that hadn't happened, hadn't even been dreamt up. But each one had a tinge of darkness to it. Each one had just a hint of death lurking in the background. I swallowed once and the visions changed, lightened. Taking one last pull, I withdrew my fangs, the warmth of healing flooding me with contentment.

Bastian's fist closed around my hair, the soft pull of it opening my eyes. His were bright and blazing, copper with a dose of power I'd thought was lost down here. "Is that what you see? Was that you?"

Confused, I shook my head. Reflexively, his fist tightened a bit more, drawing my face nearer.

"When you drink from me, is that what you see? That future? It is the future, isn't it?"

He'd never shared a vision with me before. "You saw it, too?"

Silently, he nodded, the wonder stamped all over him.

I thought of all the times I'd drunk from him and the path we'd traveled. "It's *a* future, but I only see that with you—the possibilities. I don't really know what they mean or if they'll come true. So far, though, they have."

A smile dawned on his face, the beauty of it zinging right down to my cold heart.

"Good," he murmured, pressing a soft kiss to my lips. He lingered there, tasting me in a way that made my whole body sing before breaking his mouth from mine and hauling me to my feet.

"When we get out of this, I'm taking you to bed for a month. The whole world can burn for all I care. It'll be you and me and a few of those positions you dreamt up."

I couldn't help the shiver that vibrated through my body, answering him without me saying a word.

"Glad you're on board. Now let's go find Azrael, shall we? I don't want to trek through this mess without a tour guide—no matter how unhelpful he's been."

Groaning, I let him pull me in the direction of the ruins. Maybe if we got under some decent cover, I could call for Azrael or something. Granted, the thought of that bout of good fortune made me wary.

It wasn't like we'd been lucky so far.

The trek was without incident, though every snap of a twig or flutter of a branch made us go on red alert. We'd been surprised by the harpies because Azrael hadn't thought to warn us about the dangers here.

Granted, we hadn't asked, but that was beside the point.

A chill swept through me as we entered the cover of the ruins, the cracking stone façade, and broken statues far more ominous than the open forest had been. The forest had tried to reclaim the structure. Moss and thick ivy covered most of the walls, creating a sort of canopy above us. The broken statues were all fighting poses, the metal weapons still in the cleaved arms that littered the lush floor. We picked our way through them, arriving at an open courtyard, practically brimming with more shattered marble. It reminded me a little of the Terracotta Army in China, only this army was defeated, destroyed.

"Try to call for Azrael, and then let's get out of here. This place—"

"Gives you the creeps?" I finished for him, sweeping my gaze over the pained faces of the fallen army.

"That's a word for it," he muttered, nodding.

Without wasting any more time, I called for Azrael in my mind, taking care to show him where we were. Normally, I hated when he just dropped in, but at this point I would gladly welcome him popping in from nowhere. When he didn't seem to answer the call, I opened my eyes, trepidation filling my gut.

I was stumped. What were we supposed to do now? Go find him? And did he need me saving him? If the harpies got him, he sure as hell would.

In the middle of my contemplation, a sound piqued my ears, and I grabbed Bastian so fast it was as if my body got the message a good five seconds before my brain did.

"Close your eyes," I hissed, careful not to raise my voice above the faintest hiss of a whisper.

Confused, Bastian just stared at me. Without missing a beat, I let him go and unzipped my leather jacket. Beneath it was a soft cotton undershirt, and I took the fabric in two hands and ripped it, revealing my bra and a whole lot of skin.

"While I'm enjoying the show, wha—" I put my hand over his mouth, cutting him off.

"Shut. Up," I whispered, and wrapped the mangled shirt around his eyes. "Do not move. Fuck, don't breathe. And for fuck's sake, do not take that blindfold off. No matter what."

Letting him go, I shrugged my jacket back on and zipped it up as quietly as I could. I considered pulling the dagger at my thigh, but worried I wouldn't have enough hands. I needed to lead Bastian out of here.

Said man was clutching the air trying to find me, and I gave up my debate to grab his hand.

No weapons it was.

He pulled at me, drawing me to him so he could whisper in my ear, "What is it?"

I wanted to say "Duh," but I refrained. Barely.

A shit-ton of broken statues? Check.

In the Underworld? Check.

A faint hint of a snake's rattle? Double check.

We needed to get the fuck out of here, and now, and I knew that as soon as I said one word, Bastian would be more than a little on board.

"Gorgons," I breathed in his ear, that single word making his whole spine go rigid.

Yeah, and that luck that I'd thought was *so* bad?

Well, it, too, had officially run out.

18

Those stone statues that I'd thought were creepy before? Well, as I picked through them, trying to lead Bastian clear without him stumbling or impaling himself on one of the abandoned swords, their ick-factor went up ten-fold.

Because the damn things weren't statues at all, and the utter carnage made me want to hurl.

The other thing that made me want to curl around a toilet bowl? The heavy slither of a serpent's body trailing through the high grasses and ivy. I'd never been a fan of snakes. Okay, on jewelry? Absolutely. And pythons didn't wig me out too much, but the sound of a rattle?

Hard no.

Add in the utter destruction that a gorgon's gaze

could do, and I was doing my level best to hightail it out of there. But picking through the wreckage wasn't exactly an easy task with a blind Bastian in tow. No matter how athletic or nimble he was, taking away his sight so suddenly left him frustrated and unable to adapt. I contemplated tossing him over my shoulder. I could do it, sure, but the fact of the matter was that I didn't know if I could do it and not accidentally get petrified in the process.

At the first clear spot, I took off, trying and failing to *not* let our feet pound against the dirt-strewn courtyard. Our deafening steps echoed throughout the place, summoning the rattle of one incredibly irritated snake lady. I almost tripped over my own feet as her tail whipped toward us, Bastian hanging onto me the only reason I didn't send us tumbling to the ground.

Her laugh chilled me to the bone, the throaty yet feminine chuckle both beautiful and deadly all at the same time.

"Smart of you to blindfold him," she purred, the patronizing tone a sure sign that we were cornered.

I couldn't look—not and survive—so I squeezed Bastian's hand and pressed my eyelids closed, standing as still as one of those broken statues.

"However, it is unnecessary for you to close your eyes. I don't hurt women. My stare will not affect you like it will him. Tell me, do you blindfold him because you don't trust him, or because you do?"

Confused, I kept my eyes shut, shuffling the both of us backward and away from her voice.

"You aren't the first to think of a blindfold, dear, so answer my question. Do you trust him or not?"

Croaking, I answered, "Of course I trust him."

The heavy slither of her tail got closer. "Then why the blindfold?"

Because I knew if it came to him or me, he'd choose me. Bastian would put himself in between danger and me every single time.

"It's because I do trust him that I blindfolded him. I trust him to be brave, to be strong, to put me above himself—even if it meant his death. I trust him to love me more than he loves himself, and I trust that if he were to die—in this life or the next, I wouldn't be able to make it without him."

Bastian wrapped an arm around my middle. It was just as comforting here as it had been every single other place he'd done it. "Love, remind me to slap a ring on your finger as soon as we get out of this, will you?"

Then he took advantage of my complete shock and stone-still body and whipped me behind him—getting in between me and the gorgon. My eyes popped wide, meeting a woman's gaze at the same instant. I waited for the pain, or anything that would tell me I was turning into a life-sized Sloane statue, but it didn't come.

"You weren't lying," I whispered, agog at the gorgon's beauty. It didn't matter that she had snakes writhing through her dark-auburn hair or that the bottom half of her body was encased in scales.

"About harming you? No. I could harm him, though. In fact, I really want to. So why don't you get out of my way?"

There were several stories about Medusa. Some said she'd always been a monster, just a mortal one. Some said that she'd been a priestess of Athena, and Poseidon raped her. That Athena had been so disgusted, she'd cursed her. Others said it had never been a curse, that the power to turn a man to stone had always been a gift—a way to make sure no man would ever harm her again. Given that she was trying to hurt Bastian, I figured the last two were closer to the truth.

"Please don't," I whispered, taking a step backward and shoving Bastian back with it. Raising my hands in surrender, I kept moving, shoving him away from her as best I could. "We don't want to hurt you—"

"Liar," she said, showing me fanged teeth as she smiled serenely. "If you thought it would save him, you'd chop off my head and stuff it in the darkest hole you could find."

Huffing, I conceded. "Okay, fine. But I don't want to. Does that count for anything? I don't want you dead. I don't want to cause you harm. I just want to get the hell out of here so I can send these souls to their rest, and maybe find my father in the process so I can possibly go home and have a life. I'd also like to do that without the love of my life dying on me. Is that so much to ask here? To just let us go?"

The woman—who I assumed was Medusa but didn't know for sure—let out another throaty laugh. "Oh, the gods just love you, don't they?"

I shrugged, shaking my head. "It's a mixed bag. So, what do you say? Let us out of here, and we both go our separate ways?"

Medusa gave me an assessing once-over, pursing her lips in contemplation. "You could have pulled the 'Do you know who my father is?' card but you didn't. Why?"

Snorting, I rolled my eyes. Azrael hadn't quite managed to save my ass any other time in my life, why would he start now?

Only, just as soon as I thought that, said father appeared, flaming scythe in hand and wings spread wide, landing in a crouch in between the gorgon and me. He stood, his wings shivering in agitation, leaning toward the threat as he seemed to get taller, broader, making himself a solid wall of fatherly rage.

"You will let my daughter go, Medusa, or so help me, I'll carry you to Tartarus myself."

I couldn't see her face anymore, but her simpering tone still held a big enough threat. "I want the boy, not your daughter. You know I cannot harm a female. Or Death, it seems."

Azrael growled in response, the sound making me quake in my boots, even though he was on my side. "You can't have him. Ever. Do you hear me?"

A slither was all he got in answer, but he wasn't satisfied. "Out loud, Gorgon. Swear it."

Medusa huffed, her tail rattling as it whipped in what I assumed was frustration. "*Fine.* The mage Sebastian Cartwright will not be harmed by me or my sisters by word or deed. Happy?"

"If you actually meant it, maybe. But you don't." A set of chains formed in Azrael's free hand: the two manacles barbed so they would pierce the flesh caught in them.

Her tail whipped in answer, a shuddering breath wheezing through her lungs. That's when my feet moved, getting in between her and my father, my back to her as I held out my hands to him.

"Don't." *Don't* what, I couldn't exactly say, it just felt wrong. All kinds of wrong.

Shifting to face her, I stared into her eyes. I hadn't noticed before, but her pupils were slit like a snake's, the thin irises a pretty hazel color. I'd avenged women just like her, ripped the souls from men who'd done more wrong than good, ones who had hurt people. Her gaze reminded me of the people I'd managed to save.

"Let us go. We mean you no harm and never would. Promise our passage is safe, and we'll leave in peace."

Medusa cast her gaze downward. "I swear. He will not be harmed by me or my sisters. You have earned my respect, and I would not injure you or your heart."

With that, she turned, slithering away and trailing her giant snake tail behind her.

"Thank you," I murmured to her retreating back, noticing the deep scars crisscrossing her arms and back for the first time.

Her hate for all those statues made a hell of a lot of sense. If I'd been in her shoes—or scales—I'd likely hate every person who entered my domain, too.

A touch on my shoulder made me jump, but it was only Azrael. Back to normal size and flaming scythe gone, he stared at me.

"What?"

He swallowed, before reaching out and folding me into a hug. He smelled faintly of brimstone and poppies, and I hugged him back.

"I'm glad I made it this time," he croaked, squeezing me just a little too hard.

I was, too, and it made me hate that I'd thought he wasn't right before he showed up. A stab of guilt ripped through me, and I fought off a sniffle. I would not cry, dammit, but the relief was hitting me hard.

He reluctantly let me go as I pushed away, the sorrow coloring his features plain as day. "I've done a lot of things wrong. I'm glad I got that right."

It was hard to come up with a response to that. We hadn't healed enough as a family for me to pat him on the back and give him a "good job" pep talk. But it was a start.

Clearing my throat, I managed to ask, "Where were you? We lost you in the middle of the harpy attack."

Before he could answer me, Bastian let out an irritated growl and asked, "Can I take this bloody blindfold off now?"

Both Azrael and I snorted out indelicate laughs, and I picked across the statue rubble to untie the tatters of my shirt. As soon as I saw bottle-green, he clutched me to him, kissing me so fiercely I thought the top of my head was going to pop off. He broke the kiss as he wrapped me in his arms, dropping pecks onto my hair.

"Scared the bleeding life out of me. If I weren't in the Underworld already, I would have died ten times by heart attack by now. Bloody crazy, you are, you know that?" He lifted his head. "And you," he said, staring past me to look Azrael in the eye. Bastian seemed to be gearing up to give my father a piece of his mind, but in the end, he only nodded. "Thank you for showing up when you did."

Azrael rubbed the back of his neck, his cheeks pinking. "Welcome, but I almost didn't make it. Those harpies are more vicious than I remember. You guys took off before I could reason with them, and by the time I got free, you two were in the one place you shouldn't have been."

I winced. So maybe the running was a bad idea.

"Harpies test wandering souls by keeping them from getting to the river. And Medusa is supposed to test the mettle of men, not kill all of them. Every soul —except for a special few—has to cross through here. Someone needs to talk to Hades about her."

I winced, thinking about the scars on her back. Maybe that kind of job wasn't fit for a woman who had seen as much misfortune as she had.

"You might be right," he muttered, a wave of sorrow pulling at his features.

Personally, I couldn't imagine being attacked over and over and just letting people go. Maybe keeping the men who would harm her out of Elysium was exactly where she should be. I didn't know the right answer, and it made me glad that it wasn't up to me to decide.

"Come on," Azrael said, tipping his chin to the exit. "We have a ferry waiting for us."

For the first time, I looked in the direction of his chin. An ivy-coated archway led to a shore with black waters lapping at its edges. Beached was a boat, the curled bow and stern both a serpent's head.

I swallowed, barely able to croak out a pitiful affirmative before my feet followed suit.

Elysium was just beyond the water, and with it, my parents.

Finally.

19

Tears filled my eyes as my feet touched the smooth wood of the boat's floor. A smiling ferryman pocketed the single gold coin, payment I hadn't thought to bring, but Bastian had. Since he was the only non-death deity—or deity adjacent—he'd been the only one who'd had to pay to travel down the river.

My stomach had dropped when the ferryman had asked. Of all the ways to be prepared for a trip to the Underworld, money hadn't even crossed my mind.

Those tears I'd been staunchly holding back before, slipped down my cheeks as I sat down on the polished bench, the wood worn from eons of use. Bastian sat next to me, his warmth seeping into me as all the doubts came crashing down once again.

What if the boat sinks? What if we never make it? What if—

"If you think any harder, the boat will capsize," my father muttered, sitting on the bench in front, but rather than facing the direction we were going, he chose to sit facing me.

It didn't matter that he was joking, his sly smile a testament to that fact, it still made me want to punch him. "I think it's healthy to have backup plans."

"Neurotic is more like it. You're on the ferry to Elysium for Fate's sake. Maybe take a minute to breathe before you imagine perishing in a fiery boat crash?"

In my imaginings there had been no fire, but I suspected he was taking poetic license. In response, I stuck out my tongue at him before resting my temple on Bastian's shoulder. Childish? Sure, but it was the best I had.

Azrael gave me an indulgent grin before focusing on Bastian. "You plan on spending the rest of your days with her, correct? Plan on making a life with her?"

Dear sweet mother of all that was holy. This reminded me of the times my dad had grilled my dates before deigning to let me leave with them.

Bastian only smiled at him. "I plan to marry her, to live my life such as it is with her. I plan to die with her

—whether that comes today or in a thousand years. I promised her that we'd be together until the sun stops burning and the world stops turning, and I mean to keep that promise. Is this the part where you warn me off?"

Azrael smiled wide. "No. This is the part where I give you my support because my blessing is not needed nor required. You have that, too, but it's not necessary. I'm just glad she found you—or rather, you found her. There aren't many people in this universe that I'd want for her—not many that I'd think were good enough. I'm glad you pulled your head out of your ass, mage."

Such flowery words turned crude in an instant. Yes, I really was his daughter.

"Thank you," I said, the flowery part still fitting, even if he torched it with the ass talk. My parents had never gotten the chance to meet Bastian, never got to see me settled, see me in love. I hoped they would get to see me happy—if just for a moment—like Azrael had. I wanted them to see that I was okay. That their sacrifice hadn't been for nothing.

That I'd lived—even though I was different.

I swallowed hard, casting my gaze to the glittering waters. I hoped they were happy and safe. That what my horrible brother had done hadn't scarred them.

"One thing I need to know—for my own peace of

mind," Azrael began, drawing my gaze off the horizon. "If you took this job—my job—would you be fulfilled?"

I thought of a future where I brought people to their families, where I eased the suffering of the ill and infirm. Where I confirmed the valor of a soldier or reaped an evil person before they caused further destruction. Could I do what Azrael did? I thought I could. The young ones would hurt, I was sure of it. The innocent would sting something awful. But taking those that would do harm?

Piece of cake.

Joking, I asked, "When has killing people ever been a problem for me?"

Azrael sighed, shaking his head.

"Fine. Parts of it would suck, but that's because I have a heart, okay? And as long as those who did harm found an unfortunate end, I suppose it won't be so bad."

If I got to keep my family, that is. I sent that thought to Azrael, making sure he understood. I would want to keep Bastian and Darby, the Night Watch. I'd want to stay in their lives—however long I could. Granted, by the time I took the job, most of them would be long dead, but I wanted assurances.

If I get to keep them, I'll take it. But your life—the way you lived it—was lonely. I want more than that. I deserve more.

Azrael's violet eyes welled, and he nodded once. *You shall have it, my daughter. All you want for you and yours is in your grasp.*

This was the first time Azrael had spoken inside my head, and his voice had the same tenor as Hades, the vibrations nearly rattling my whole body. Smiling, I rested my head on Bastian's shoulder, letting the breeze kiss my face as the boat cut through the water.

Before I knew it, Bastian was shaking me awake. The boat was beached on a rocky shore, the littering pebbles winking at me in the bright sun. He pulled me to standing, steadying me as I climbed out of the boat.

Beyond the water's edge was a gleaming city surrounded by little pockets of odd-colored sky. I didn't understand at first until I rubbed the sleep from my eyes and really looked. What I thought were pockets were small little worlds, little heavens, each one as singular as the people who resided there. They each dotted the horizon in a glittering mass of worlds, too many for my brain to count.

How were we supposed to find my parents—or even Killian for that matter—in all of this? And the souls inside me? Would they know where to go?

Bastian gave my hand a reassuring squeeze, leading me to a large information sign that would hopefully give us some sort of direction.

"If you think this is bad, you should see Hell. It's a certified mess there and all the rings? No, thank you," Azrael said, shuddering. "I stay on the outskirts if I can help it."

Good information to be sure, but it didn't help me find what I needed. I stared at the sign—the directions were more confusing than I'd thought they'd be. My parents' names weren't anywhere on it.

I fought back tears as the world ebbed and flowed around me, the hopelessness hitting me exactly where I was sore. Swallowing down tears, I turned to Azrael. "Maybe we should let these souls out. If I can't find my parents or Darby's dad, at least I can do that."

Azrael nodded before wincing. "This is going to hurt, but you'll heal fast here."

"Wha—"

Before I really understood, he grabbed my hands with one of his and drew a blade from his hip with the other. In an instant, I felt the slashing pain of his knife meeting my flesh, and then the burning ache of the souls escaping their prison. Granted, I much appreciated that it didn't feel like my entire body was being flash fried, but I couldn't say it was altogether comfortable, either.

The scream that escaped me had the residents of Elysium crowding around us, the offers to help drowned out by my pain. And then it was over, the metallic sigils still there, but the full ache in my hands gone.

Confused and more than a little sweaty, I rested against Bastian as he gave withering looks at my father.

"Was that necessary? You could have warned her."

Azrael shrugged. "I thought it was better to treat it like a Band-Aid—the ring's wards kept the souls contained, but there wasn't a better way to get them out other than just cutting the skin."

Bastian huffed. "Like you've ever ripped off a plaster a day in your life. Fun fact: it hurts no matter how you do it. The quick way is just more traumatizing."

Azrael sucked in a breath through his teeth, wincing. "Sorry."

I was stuck on the sigils still burned into the skin of my palms. At my questioning gaze, Azrael shrugged. "It marks you as one of mine. It actually could have gotten you past the harpies and gorgon, but I forgot it was there. Usually I have my ring, and that grants me passage, but…" He shrugged, trailing off.

He'd given me safe passage and left himself without? If my brain wasn't so addled, I could have asked him why, but I was just so tired. I had to think that was a bad thing—being tired in the Underworld. I'd already slept once, and that had been with a host of souls in my body.

I stared at the information board—the text just as confusing now as it had been before I released the souls. I mean, I was dead, right? Shouldn't it be at least a little helpful? We were in heaven, weren't we?

Honestly, I was about to throw a full-on tantrum when Bastian came through with logic.

"Why don't we ask someone?" Bastian asked, frowning at the tremendously useless information board. "There has to be someone here who knows where your parents are or where Killian is, right?"

He transferred my weight to Azrael, who clutched me to him like he was close to absorbing me.

"I'm tired," I muttered, my head lolling up to look at his face.

"I know. Shouldn't be too long now, and you'll be right as rain."

"That sounds bad," I slurred, having a hard time holding my head up. "Am I dying again?"

It wouldn't be the first time, but since I was in the Underworld, this time it would probably stick.

My father looked down at me, glittering lights surrounding his head as a smile bloomed across his features. "Not dying. Changing. It won't be long now."

"I'm scared," I breathed, the fear making it hard to

draw in my next breath. Or maybe my lungs just weren't working, I couldn't tell.

"Don't be. It's been a long time coming. I'm sorry, Sloane. I thought we'd have more time. I thought I'd be able to show you everything you needed to know. But I want you to know you were loved and wanted. And I've never been prouder than I am of you and your sister. Will you tell her that for me? When you see her again? Will you tell her that I love her, that I never regretted a day being your father?"

My sluggish brain didn't understand, my body hanging in Azrael's grip as his eyes pleaded for me to listen. "You sound like you're saying goodbye. Are you leaving?"

Was that my voice all childlike and small? Had I ever sounded like that?

"Not leaving, but you will eventually. You'll continue being the beautiful woman you've become. You'll tie your life with the man you love. You'll be a sister and a friend, you'll have a full long life, and I fear I won't be around for it. For either of you. I know I haven't been the father you needed, but I'm glad you both had some mighty fine men to take my spot. I'm glad you learned the lessons I couldn't teach you. And that you both found love when I couldn't bless you with that, either."

Fear clutched tight to my middle. "I don't want you to go."

His smile was wobbly, or maybe that was the tears in my eyes—I didn't know which. This felt horrible, like I was losing someone else, like I was losing a part of me.

"I'm not going anywhere. I'll always be with you," he whispered, kissing my forehead.

But that felt like a comforting lie, and I was too tired to make him tell me the truth.

20

At the touch of Azrael's lips to my skin, a flood of what I could only describe as life filled me, solidifying my legs and straightening my spine. He'd done the same thing to Darby what felt like ages ago, healing her in a way I'd never seen before.

Had I been dying like she'd been? Azrael said I wasn't, but a part of me didn't believe him.

I didn't know what was going on, but my bullshit meter was going off big time.

Azrael gave me another tired smile. "You'll know when you know, kid. Don't be so quick to find all the answers. They'll come when they're supposed to."

What a cryptic and patronizing answer, Dad.

"I like you calling me Dad. Did you know that?"

Blinking, the weight of that statement hit me like a bomb. "No," I croaked. "I didn't."

"I found him," Bastian announced as he jogged back to us. "Not your parents, but one of those souls knows Killian. I figure we can check in on him, and he might know something, or we can ask someone else. What do you say?"

Truth be told, we probably should have left as soon as those souls were freed, but the carrot of helping my sister was almost too big to say no to. I looked at Azrael, his skin not nearly as vibrant as usual.

"What do you think? You said Essex could be coming to attack the house. Should we go back?" But he hadn't said that, had he? Simon said he'd seen it in his mind.

Azrael shook his head as he moved farther down a busy street, the foot traffic almost swallowing him up as he weaved through the souls. "Not yet. We still have time. Let's go see him."

Reluctantly, Bastian and I followed, the worry in my gut multiplying with every passing second. Catching up to Azrael, Bastian instructed him to take a left at the next street. We followed the directions Bastian had been given, arriving at a neighborhood that looked very familiar. It resembled the one I'd grown up in, the scent of hot dogs cooking on a grill and roses blooming a heady perfume of home. Ten houses down, we came to a pretty white house with a black mailbox. The name "Adler" was lettered neatly, but there were two pairs of handprints, one a man's size and one a little girl's.

I swallowed hard, debating on whether or not I had the courage to do this. If I could even get through talking to the man who'd raised my sister without bawling my fucking eyes out. Bastian nudged me with his elbow, jutting his chin at Azrael. He was paler than he'd been just a few minutes ago, and now he was wobbling on his feet.

I reached for him, but he lurched away, the door to Killian's house his heading. We followed, and I thought we might have to catch him if he fell.

What had he done?

Before we reached the door, it swung open, Darby's father filling the entrance. His blond hair was slightly messy, and he had on a ratty college sweater over jeans, with a pair of comfy slippers on his feet. His face fell a bit when he saw me, and it made my heart ache just a little.

"Mr. Adler? Killian?"

I'd only seen him the once, and he'd been bloody and bruised. The man before me barely resembled the one on the lakeshore, what seemed like so long ago.

"Yes?"

"Umm…" I trailed off, swallowing a lump in my throat. "My name is Sloane. I—I know your daughter, Darby. Well, she's my sister."

Killian seemed confused for just a moment before he invited us in. We piled inside his neat little living room, taking chairs when we were offered a seat.

"Wow. I didn't think I'd meet any of Darby's siblings." Killian pulled at his ear, a sign or nervousness as his gaze kept falling to Azrael. "Good to see you again, though you have looked better. Would you like some tea or something?"

Azrael gave him a weak smile. "No need. I'll feel better soon."

That felt like a lie, and I wasn't the only one who thought so. Bastian and Killian shared a glance that both said they thought my father was full of shit. I had to agree.

"I'm sorry to bother you," I began, trying to figure out what to say. Funny, we'd traveled all this way, and now I was trying to figure out my script?

Way to go, Sloane.

"It's just, I was coming here anyway, and I thought you might want to give me a message to give her since you two didn't get a chance to say goodbye."

There was more. Like how I was sorry we hadn't been able to save him. I was sorry that the plan had failed him—that we hadn't thought to save him sooner. I wanted to tell him that Darby was going to be okay—that we'd be there for her.

Killian's smile was watery, and he nodded. "I—I'd love to give her a message. But… is she okay? I know she isn't. No one would be after that. So much became clear after. All of Mariana's spells lifted, and I saw the life we had before she left. I can't think of a better gift to be given than the time I got with Darby—the life we built. She grew into such a beautiful woman. If you don't mind, I'd like to write her a note?"

I blinked, surprised I hadn't thought of something so simple. "Of course. Take your time."

Killian stood, pacing over to a rolltop desk and began scribbling on a legal pad. While he did that, I returned to my inspection of Azrael. His skin was now solidly in the gray range, his black hair fading to white before my very eyes. His irises began to get a purple quality to them as he continued to study his hands. It was as if he was losing his glamour.

That couldn't be good.

I flicked my eyes to Bastian, and he, too, was staring at Azrael, like he might turn into a pillar of salt at any moment. Bastian must have sensed my stare because we then shared a worried glance.

What was going on? One second, he was fine, and the next he was like this.

Killian rustled some papers, ripping them from the legal pad and folding them together. He rose from the desk chair, his warm blue eyes on me. "I can't thank you enough for doing this," he croaked, his eyes getting watery. "If this doesn't work, could you just tell her I'm proud of her?"

I hadn't even considered Killian's note not working, but the reality of it was too probable to discount. "Of course I will."

Azrael rose shakily, almost stumbling as he lurched toward Killian and grabbed his hand. "I said it before, but it bears repeating. Thank you for being her father. Thank you for raising her. Thank you for the sacrifices you made. I'll never forget it."

Killian surrounded Azrael's hand with both of his, a sort of knowledge coming over his face that I didn't understand. "It was my honor."

Azrael gave him a jerky nod, straightening. He seemed to gather himself and turned. His gait was smoother, a little less fragile than before. And he walked right out of Killian's house, leaving the three of us to stare after him.

"Is he going to be all right?" Killian asked, and I

couldn't peel my gaze off the now-closed door to answer him.

"I'm sure he'll be right as rain soon enough," Bastian replied, doing what I couldn't.

Because I didn't know if Azrael would be okay, and I didn't know why he'd deteriorated or how someone like him would decline so quickly.

"It was good to talk to you, Killian, but I fear we must be off."

I heard Bastian say those words, but all I could do was stare at that damn door, only breaking my gaze to bid Killian a hasty goodbye. Bastian gently latched onto my elbow and guided me to the stoop. But once we got there, I could hear things I most definitely should *not* be able to hear.

Especially from the man I was listening to.

Just a little longer. I can make it a little longer. Stupid Fate. Why couldn't she have thrown me a bone on this one? I just wanted... It doesn't matter what I wanted. But Sloane won't understand that it was meant to be, that my choices were limited. That my failures were the rules I'd been given.

I couldn't breathe. I couldn't swallow. I couldn't do anything but listen to that litany and let the knowledge that something was really, really fucking wrong wash over me. Shaking myself, I managed to snap out of it, and a bout of rage flashed through me like a brushfire.

"Why are you cursing Fate? And why in the high holy fuck can I read you? *What* did you do?"

He'd kissed my forehead just like he'd done to Darby. A gentle little flutter against my skin and then I'd felt better. But unlike with Darby, Azrael looked like he was dying.

Was he dying? Could he even die?

"I told you," Azrael responded, giving me one of his patented raised eyebrows. "You're changing. And don't read my thoughts—it's rude."

I blinked at him for a solid five seconds before my eye started twitching. "Says the man who has read nearly all of my thoughts in every single interaction we've ever had. But you never answered the Fate part. Why are you cursing Fate, and what did you do?"

Just a little longer. Just a little longer. Just a little longer.

"Why do you keep saying that?"

Azrael shook his head, but the act made him almost stumble. He reached out a hand, using a cute white picket fence to keep himself vertical. "I told you not to read my thoughts."

"And I told you to stuff it. It seems we're at an impasse on that front."

He cleared his throat—or at least he tried to. That turned into a cough that racked his whole body and almost took him to his knees. Bastian and I lunged for him, easing him to the sidewalk as we waited for him to catch his breath.

I barely held in a sob as I watched a god withering away right before my eyes. "What is going on?"

He gave me a halfhearted chuckle. "Just my past catching up to me."

I didn't understand until I saw a flash of white hair out of the corner of my eye. I could feel him, his presence like a black spot on my brain. "He was never going to attack the house, was he?"

Azrael smiled. "You're entirely too smart for your own good, you know that? Help me up?"

Bastian and I pulled Azrael to standing, his touch sipping just a little of the power he'd bestowed on me.

Just a little. You'll get it back. Just need to look strong for a second.

Then he shoved me, hard. Hell, it was practically a throw. My ass hit the pavement as the glitter of a familiar blade cut the air right where I'd been standing just a moment before.

"Ruining my fun again, old man?" my brother growled, brandishing the same blade that had taken my life and so many others. "No matter. I have plenty of people to kill."

Then the world slowed, and my heart stopped, and the sun died. Because Essex flicked that blade out again, the point aimed for Bastian's throat. But then Bastian wasn't there anymore—he'd sailed over the fence Azrael had just used to prop himself up.

And in his stead stood my father with Essex's blade buried in his chest.

21

At first, what I was seeing didn't make any sense. It just couldn't. There was no way Essex Drake—the man who'd murdered me and my parents and so many others—could just come down here and steal from me. There was no way he could just try and kill me again.

No way he could take this much.

I stood there, frozen—when I'd gotten to my feet, I couldn't say—watching as Essex held the hilt of the blade, his eyes wide with an emotion I couldn't track before it morphed into a sneer. The blip of pain there and gone in an instant.

"A little out of order, but it will make things easier on the back end, I think. How does it feel, Father? To know that I will take all your children from you? To know that I got my revenge?" His lip quivered, the unmitigated joy playing havoc with the muscles of his face. "Tell me, did you realize when you stole my children—my wife—from me that this day would come? Did Fate tell you when you would be reaped, too?"

Azrael latched onto Essex's hand—the one still holding the hilt—and stepped forward, pressing the blade farther into his body. "Do you think I don't know your game, boy? I know all about your deal with Nemesis. Did you think my sister wouldn't tell me?" Azrael let out a low chuckle, a wet cough drawing blood to his lips. "She agreed to your proposal and gave you safe passage here because Fate deigned it so. You are not in charge of destiny any more than I am. And I did not *take* your family from you. You did that when you started killing your own." Then he lifted his chin, nodding to a woman and child as they stood staring in shock at the tableau.

"Essex?" the woman called before she covered her mouth with her hand, disgust making her shake her head. Her dress seemed straight out of the Middle Ages, with belled sleeves and an outer, more durable dress corseted over a lighter under layer. Her hair was a deep red, the curly strands threaded through with flowers and braids. She even had a haphazard flower crown that was staying on her head by a wing and a prayer, the handiwork of the child at her side.

The little girl was a copy of her mother except for her hair, the strands a familiar shade of white. She held daisies and dahlias and roses in her little hand, squishing the stems as she stared at what I could only assume was her father.

Essex looked, just for a second, before he did a double take.

"Bronwyn? Clara?" He shook his head as if the sight of the pair was something he'd never thought he'd see in a million years. "I—I don't understand."

"What have you done?" she asked, aghast as she moved the little girl behind her skirts, the girl's flowers forgotten on the cobblestone road.

Shakily, Essex turned back to Azrael, confusion and pain and rage amalgamating throughout his whole body. "How?"

"Did you think I wouldn't care for them? They were yours, and I couldn't prevent their deaths, but I could keep them safe. All you had to do was wait—your time was coming. You would have been with them soon enough. And now you have made it so this is the last time you'll see them—see all of them."

Several people stepped forward, each one staring at

Essex with hurt on their faces. Whispers of their thoughts flitted through my mind like Azrael's had, memories of their deaths, the pain they'd felt at his hand. Sweeping my eyes over the crowd, I could see so many. So many deaths, so much torment, so many people lost.

And he had been the author of it all.

This crowd, this moment was just the beginning of his punishment. This was the knife in his heart. Because he would never see his family again, and after what he had done, they didn't want a single thing to do with him, anyway.

Quick as a flash, Azrael reached out and wrapped his fingers around Essex's throat, his other hand still on the hilt of the blade in his chest. Brilliant bright light peaked from under my father's fingers as Essex's pallor grayed slightly. It took a second, but he finally got the gumption to yank himself away, leaving his blade in our father's chest—watching with a chaotic mind of sorrow and regret and avarice.

I saw the instant he chose himself—the exact second Essex realized he had nothing to hold onto anymore. He stumbled, staggered, and then he took off running, damn near disappearing in the crowd. I stood frozen for a moment, unsure if I should keep him from escaping or—

"Go, Sloane. I've got Azrael," Bastian shouted, giving me the answer I needed.

Essex had always put his revenge over everything else. I refused to follow in his footsteps. Instead of following my brother, I pointed my feet toward Bastian and Azrael.

"What are you doing?" Azrael croaked, blood coating his pale lips as it leaked from the side of his mouth. "He'll get away."

I shook my head as I gave him a wobbly smile. "No, he won't," I insisted, brushing a strand of hair from Azrael's face. "He's headed for a gate. I'll catch up to him soon enough."

"You—you're staying with me?"

His voice was so small, so vulnerable, it opened my chest wide and left me bleeding. A smattering of glass was where my heart should have been, the damage too great to ever be repaired. I sucked in a shuddering breath, the words to comfort him lodged in my throat.

But I could count on Bastian.

"We both are," he said, assuring Azrael, who was getting paler by the second. "We wouldn't leave you alone."

Azrael's odd violet gaze shifted from me to the man I loved. "I'm glad she has you." A wet cough seized his chest, sending spasms throughout his whole body. His eyes rolled back in his head before he managed to find himself again, those eyes that matched my own, focusing what would likely be the last time.

"You knew, didn't you?" I whispered, the weight of it all crashing down on me at once. "That this was going to happen when you brought me here. That—"

Azrael's smile was sad. "I've never been one to argue with Fate. Maybe you'll be better at that than me." He swallowed thickly, before spearing me with a gaze that was so final, I felt it in my bones. "Better do this now before I run out of time. Love you and your sister. Remember to tell her."

I was in the process of nodding when his hand found my throat much like he'd done to Essex. Only he didn't seem to steal anything from me. No, he gave me something. My entire body buzzed with power, with knowledge, with a vitality that seemed almost too much for my skin to contain.

Memories—his—raced through my mind. What he had seen, what he'd done. What I was now. He'd been right this whole time—he'd had to follow the rules because his fate had been sealed.

But mine wasn't.

An itch bloomed in my back, almost making me cry out, the need to keep my eyes on Azrael the only thing that kept me upright. The irritation turned into a burn, and that burn morphed into a pain so fierce that the urge to scream was almost too much to bear. A blisteringly hot ache settled through me, and with it, a weight that nearly brought me over backward. A shiver worked its way through me, starting at my head and flowing all the way down to my toes, and all the way out to—

I shifted, the black things racing just out of my field of vision as I turned. My hand went to my shoulder, the feathers there smooth and soft and—

There are feathers on my back. I have wings. There are wings on my back. Actual wings.

I stared down at the man who had given me life— twice—my gaze landing on the smile frozen on his lips. My stomach lurched, my heart—the one I'd thought was just broken—shattered even more. He was gone. And I couldn't bring him back, and I couldn't deal my way out of it, and I—

A sob ripped up my throat, the agony of loss more than I could bear. My fingers closed around the hilt of the blade, ripping the offending thing from him so I could clutch him to me. My mother had done this same thing, held my lifeless body to her chest. I'd thought that memory hurt, but this…

A hand found my shoulder, a tiny one that I had no choice but to answer. Clara Drake stood there, tears on her small face. Her mother stood with the child's hand in hers. Bronwyn swallowed hard, a sob almost leveling her. When she could speak, she asked, "Can I—can we say goodbye to him?"

Thoughts raced through me. Clara and Azrael sitting in a meadow, her weaving flowers in his white hair. He didn't glamour himself with the child, and she'd loved playing with it because it matched hers. But it wasn't just Clara. It was all of them. It was our family, and each of them wanted to say goodbye.

"We'll take care of him," Clara insisted. "I'll take him to the field. He likes the flowers there."

There was no way to say no, so I nodded, moving away from Azrael as the others filled the gap I left. Bastian came to me, holding me up as the sorrow threatened to pull me all the way under.

"Sloane, look at me."

Doing so almost gutted me, but I did it. But for the first time, those bottle-green eyes weren't the balm they usually were.

"We need to go after Essex."

Yes, we did need to do that. Too bad I didn't know if I could.

"Love, I need you to remember the family you have left. He'll steal them, too, if we don't get moving."

And that's all it took. I latched onto Bastian's hand,

and we took off running, pushing faster as we sprinted through the city with a singular focus.

It turned out we had an easier go of it than Essex had. The crowd parted for us, but had refused for him. Hell, some of them threw their shoulders into him on purpose, hurling food and objects at him. One soul even started beating him with her umbrella. Essex stumbled, digging in his pockets as he tried to run, the sound of his chaotic mind a whirling mess of blame and toxic thoughts.

He still thought he could get back to the gate. Thought he could win. Sure, he hadn't accomplished all he needed to, but there was still time.

Wrong on all counts, buddy.

Then he found whatever it was that he'd been searching for, yanking it from his pocket like he'd struck gold. With a twist to his fingers, he winked out of sight, popping up in a clear spot of the street fifty yards ahead.

Motherfucker.

I'd only seen that power in one other person, a sorcerer that I'd chased all over the ass-end of Tennessee. My eye practically twitched as I remembered the man I'd had to chase up a water tower just to trap.

I hated heights.

Pushing faster, we shortened the gap, sprinting like the hounds of Hell were after us. We'd almost gotten close enough to reach him when he turned that fucking dial again. Only this time he didn't just end up fifty yards ahead. He was so far away, there was no way we'd be able to catch him—not if he did that again.

Essex turned to look at us and twisted it again, winking out of sight. Shaking, I tried to make my mind focus on the task at hand.

Essex. Running. Now.

Those feathery extensions on my back got the message before I did, flapping once and shooting me— and by extension, Bastian—into the air like a goddamn javelin.

Did I mention I was not good with heights?

My stomach lurched, threatening to evict every- thing in it as I stared in horror at the ground that was *much* too far away for my liking. My eyes managed to find Bastian's, his body hanging from my lone hand.

This was not safe. *What if I drop him, what if… The gate. Essex is heading for the gate.*

I saw it in my mind, the stone walls and arched ceil- ing. The near-constant *drip, drip, drip* of water that made me equally creeped out and have to pee all at the same time. I wanted to go there—needed it more than air in my lungs—wanted Bastian's feet firmly planted on the ground. And then it was as if I was holding my breath —like every molecule of oxygen had been sucked from my lungs, as I was squeezed in a vice so tight I thought my eyes would pop from their sockets.

When I could breathe again, I sucked in huge gasps of cool, musty air, my brain just not comprehending the fact that we were standing in the middle of the too-long hallway that led to the Underworld.

Bastian's groan was music to my ears as I reached for him with both hands, hysterical laughter bubbling up my chest as adrenaline flooded my body. We were on the ground, he was alive, and the gate was close. The pounding of footsteps echoed through the corridor, their vibration a siren call of vengeance.

They pulled me to my feet, and I followed them— or at least I tried to. Those wings that had been so awesome before—*not*—didn't exactly fit in this hallway, the scrape of the wall yanking feathers out at the root. What had Azrael done to make them go away? That last time I'd seen him with wings, he'd just shivered a little, and they had gone *poof*. Emulating this was marginally successful, the things tucking up and back instead of disappearing all the way, but I'd take it.

"Almost there, love," Bastian growled, his thirst for justice just as big as mine.

Those steps were so close, I could practically taste

the blood on my tongue. I wouldn't swallow it, but the thought of ripping Essex's throat out was a balm to my soul. We rounded a corner, the largest turn in the whole stretch of the corridor so near to the entrance it made my entire body shudder and my stomach drop.

Essex was in our home.

Again.

Pushing as fast as I could, I let go of Bastian's hand as we came to the end of the hall. Essex had just busted through the door, diving for the cleaver on Simon's macabre altar table as soon as he saw it.

Essex brandished it like the weapon it was, and Simon and Dahlia stumbled back. The bastard had caught them by surprise, but what he hadn't accounted for was my sister. While Simon and Dahlia backed away, Darby pulled a gun from her hip and fired without a second's hesitation. Essex moved at the last second, so her shot wasn't lethal, but it caught him in the shoulder.

Still, it had the intended result. Essex dropped the cleaver, his hand no longer able to hold the blade, and then he was on his ass.

And then *I* was on *him*, flying out of that hall like a missile. I landed just like a harpy, feet down, my boots pounding into his gut with a satisfying squish. Reaching down, I snatched him from the floor, raising him up above my head, fangs bared.

I was going to rip his throat out and watch him bleed out on this floor. Then when he was well and truly dead, I was going to try and conjure some of those chains Azrael had tried to capture Medusa with and haul his sorry soul down to Tartarus. And if I needed help, I'd ask Hades or Persephone.

Yes, that was precisely what I was going to do.

"Sloane?" Darby breathed, only slightly pulling my focus from the man who'd earned every bit of pain I was going to dish out. "Sloane!"

"What? I'm a little busy here," I griped, turning my chin to stare at my sister.

Her hands were raised over her head, her gun being taken from its holster by an incredibly tall man in a suit. There were others in the room as well, men and women I didn't know, who were frisking Simon and Dahlia for weapons, and others who were holding giant orbs of magic like they were cocking a gun. Thomas and Axel were in magical cuffs, and Bishop was face-down on the floor, an agent's knee on his back and magical ropes around his arms. Another agent pointed an odd-looking gun at Bastian, a canister of glowing liquid at its base that looked very familiar. My brain caught up and I recognized it as a very powerful sleeping potion.

A slight gentleman with a purple paisley tie cleared his throat, stepping forward like he was in charge. Maybe he was.

"As I stated before while you were otherwise indisposed: Arcane Bureau of Investigation. You're all under arrest."

22

I had a feeling no one in the history of the ABI had laughed at Director August Theodore Davenport III, but there I was, cackling like a lunatic as I still held Essex by the neck. Tears almost poured out of my eyes as the hilarity hit me full force.

"Fates, you are adorable," I said, wiping my eyes. "Hate to break it to you, but unless your jurisdiction covers deities, you're shit out of luck."

Davenport scrunched his nose like he smelled something rotten. "Deity," he said scathingly. "And what deity are you supposed to be? The god of vampires? Or maybe you're one of those new gods that presides over avocado toast or something."

The ABI Director appeared around my age, but his mind was much older. I'd peg him around the eight or nine hundred range. Still, he sounded like a damn Boomer.

I flashed him my fangs, my wings spreading wide. "Tell me—have you ever heard of the Angel of Death? Don't answer that. I know you have. Well, Essex and I are his kids. He used to have a bunch, but Essex here killed them all. Even me. But see, Daddy didn't like that, and he brought me back." I turned my chin, staring Essex down. "All that power that you wanted, that you killed for, that you tried to steal? Belongs to me now."

I flicked my gaze back to Davenport. "So no, I won't be put under arrest, and neither will my friends. And Essex here, well, his time is up. I'm going to rip out his throat and watch him bleed. Then I'm going to chain his soul and haul his ass down to Tartarus. And if I see so much as a flicker of one of those spells, I'll take every single one of you down with him."

The other agents in the room seemed to get the message far faster than their boss, the orbs of magic winking out of sight and the guns properly stowed as each one took a collective step away from my friends.

"You can't be Death," Davenport countered like he was the end all be all of god assignments.

I smiled, letting just a hint of power leak out of my eyes. "I can, and I am."

He sputtered, shaking his head. "But Azrael—"

"Do. Not. Speak of my father as if you know him, August. You do not. I know in your precious little head, you think of him as a confidant or a shoulder to cry on, but I can assure you, Azrael is retired."

And retired was a nicer way of putting what Essex had done to him. My stomach pitched, and I tightened my grip on my brother's throat, the pain of saying goodbye to Azrael far sharper than I ever thought it would be.

"I suggest you stand down, Director, and remember where you are. This is the entrance to the Underworld. You're in my house, so to speak."

"But... but you're a murderer," he cried, staring at me like he hadn't meant to blurt that out.

I scoffed, enjoying the little choking sounds Essex was making. "So are you, but if it makes you feel better, think of it as on-the-job training."

Davenport got really flustered then, like a toddler about to throw a fit. "You can't kill him. We need him."

"Oh, I assure you, I can, and I will." Inspecting the director's thoughts, though, I decided to expose the meat of the issue. "But what, pray tell, do you need this miserable, lying, murdering sack of dog shit for? Plan to install him in your newest ABI branch and let him run amuck? Maybe kill a few more agents, break a few more prisoners out of jail, conspire with Director O'Shea to open a goddamn rift in the planet so she can steal the power of the dead? What the fuck could you need him for?"

Davenport's shoulders fell in defeat. "He has answers. Knows who's dirty. Who's been bribed to keep their mouths shut. He knows where the bodies are buried."

And they wanted him alive so he could dish, sleeping in a nice cushy cell with cable TV and a nice comfy mattress. I didn't think so. "No deal, sorry. I've seen the way your agency runs its prisons, and they leave something to be desired. You can't keep hold of the prisoners you've got."

Davenport ground his teeth, his brain grasping at straws to sweeten the deal. And make no mistake, he was making a deal—he just didn't know it yet. "Essex Drake would not be going to prison. He would go to a black site, sedated with enough sleeping potion to kill a fucking rhino, and strapped to a table until his brain has been mined of every detail, secret, and cover-up for the last four centuries. Then, you may do with him what you wish."

"I can do what I wish now," I said, yawning. "What's in it for me?"

Davenport growled under his breath before sucking

in air through his nose like an irritated Southern mother. "Fine," he ground out. "I will expunge the records of Agents Bishop La Roux and Sarina Kenzari, releasing them from their contracts if they so wish. I will grant immunity to Darby Adler for her crimes against the Knoxville coven and the Monroe nest. She will be deputized as the new Warden of Knoxville and will accept the duties that entails. Also, I will grant blanket immunities for all past crimes to Sebastian and Simon Cartwright, Dahlia St. James, Harper Jones, Axel Monroe, Thomas Gao, Emrys Zane, and that little revenant girl ya'll keep in the kitchen."

He almost had everything, so I lowered Essex to the floor. He was turning an awful shade of purple, anyway.

"Get it to me in writing within the hour." My mama—and every episode of *Law & Order*—didn't raise no fool. "Binding contract that states you may not have possession of Essex Drake for longer than one month, his body and soul to be claimed by me and only me."

"Done." He'd given too much away too quickly, and he knew it.

"And Davenport?"

He winced, his shoulders hunching.

"One more thing."

It made me sick to my stomach, but Bastian and I returned to the Underworld empty-handed. The fact that I got Davenport to agree to publicly acknowledge every agent and civilian Essex had murdered, and pay their surviving families reparations for up to one century, still didn't make me feel any better. Sure, it was the absolute least they could do, and agencies were typically stingy with the pennies, but inside I wanted to curl around a toilet and evict my lunch.

I had not even an inkling of what I might be walking into, and I didn't think my heart could handle it.

"If you think any harder, you're going to explode and we've already got the wings to deal with," Bastian chided, fitting his arm around my waist as we walked into the building, my wings barely fitting through the double doors.

The last time Bastian and I had been to this building, we'd entered from a very different door. This time we took the direct route. A smiling doorman skirted around a counter, reaching for my hand with both of his. He shook mine once before moving to Bastian's.

"Sloane, Sebastian, it is so good to see you. Mistress Persephone had me set aside your keys for you and asked that I show you to your apartment. It's one floor down from theirs." He said this *sotto voce* like this was a very big deal. I had a feeling it really was.

He pressed the golden call button, and the elevators opened. I stared at the too-small elevator and then looked at my shoulder.

"Meet you guys there?"

Bastian's gaze had the same track mine had. "Yes, that might be best."

Snorting at the absurdity of it, I kissed his lips.

"See you in a minute." Then I walked right back out the doors, letting the wings I couldn't figure out how to put away haul me up to the second highest floor in the tallest building I'd ever seen in my life.

Good times.

"Are you kidding me?" I hissed, trying for the fifth time to follow the instructions Hermes had written down, but his handwriting was so bad it was no wonder doctors everywhere had the worst penmanship. "Can't I get the training wheels version?"

"Oh, for Fate's sake," Persephone muttered, slapping her book down on my new couch. "I'll read it." She snatched up the paper I had been helplessly trying to decipher, took one look at it and yelled at the top of her lungs, "Hermes!"

A fine-boned man with the body of a long-distance runner appeared a second later. Dressed in a gold caftan and a wide-brimmed hat—a completely different outfit from what he was wearing an hour ago —he minced to Seph with a smile on his face.

"You rang?"

She waved the paper at him. "What is this? No one can read your handwriting, you weirdo."

"Those are detailed instructions."

"That no one can read."

It had been four hours, a very inventive round of grief sex, and a messy bath, and I was completely done with these wings already. The only upside to the damn things was that they didn't tear my clothes—*don't ask me how*—and they made drying after a bath a snap. Yes, there was currently a mess of feathers everywhere in our new bathroom, but who needed towels?

"Can you just walk me through it step by step?" I asked, praying he would decide to help.

Hermes checked his watch, counted on all of his fingers, and then shrugged. "I've got three minutes, so I'll take this slow."

Three minutes was slow?

He snapped his fingers in my face. "Focus. Take a

deep breath and let it out. Then imagine the wings disappearing into your back. When I first got mine, I pictured it all horror-movie style with the cracking ribs and blood and stuff. They winked right out of sight, no muss, no fuss."

My expression was skeptical, but he nodded at me. "Promise. The more gruesome the better."

I followed his advice, complete with the bones snapping and blood flying, and wouldn't you know it? The weight of them disappeared almost instantly.

"Look at you," he exclaimed, latching onto my hands and spreading them wide. "A quick study. Okay, I've got to run. I'll see you guys at the coronation later, though, okay?"

I swallowed thickly and nodded.

Coronation.

Had I known when I took this job that there was an actual ceremony involved, I might have skipped it. Just the thought of me in public, in a dress, in front of a boatload of actual gods? It sounded like the worst form of torture. But someone—*Seph*—promised me food, and I was a sucker for a good buffet.

Plus, they were unveiling Azrael's statue, and if nothing else, that needed to be celebrated.

A god dying was rare, so rare, in fact, that the entirety of the Underworld mourned the loss of Azrael with a passion that warmed me a little. In his mind he hadn't been loved or wanted, but with the vehemence in which these people grieved him, I knew that just wasn't true.

Azrael's statue would reside in the Elysium fields, a monument to all those he had brought to peace.

Then I would be paraded around as the new Angel of Death, which sounded like the absolute worst thing I could think of *ever*.

"Oh, it won't be that bad," Seph said, elbowing me in the side. "You look beautiful, your lover is hotter than blazes, and you've been promised as many appetizers as your stomach can hold. What more is there?"

I thought about all the worries I had stockpiled in my brain, but most of them centered around the very alive man I wanted to spend the rest of eternity with. The one that I wanted to see happy and free and not trapped down here.

Seph seemed to see the worries on my face. "Is it Bastian? Are you worried about him?"

I swallowed. I couldn't decide if he should live down here or up there. Couldn't figure out if being down here was going to hurt him or not. And what if something happened to his brother or any of our friends while we were gone?

Seph waved her hand like she was shooing my

extremely valid worries away. "Oh, please. Why did you think I made him eat the fruit salad? I even told him I made it myself, so he had two helpings to make sure I knew he liked it."

Confused, I took a step back. "I don't know. Why did you make him eat the fruit salad?"

She smiled like I was cute. "It had pomegranate seeds in it. *Underworld* pomegranate seeds." She specifically stressed the "Underworld" part, but I shrugged. Rolling her eyes, she elaborated. "It makes it so he can come and go whenever he wants. You're welcome."

I sputtered, "But that was before Azrael—"

"Fate and I are good buddies. She filled me in. So quit worrying about it already, and get out of that bathrobe. We have a party to get to."

That "party" turned into a three-day event, complete with the statue unveiling, my coronation, and an incredibly raucous after-party that made me glad I was already dead so I couldn't experience the hangover.

Fun fact: when you were a new god, everyone wanted to buy you drinks, and these people must have had iron stomachs, petrified livers, or both.

"Where are you taking me?" I asked as I let Bastian

lead me by the hand down a manicured street. I hadn't started my duties yet, but Hades had told me to take a few days, that the dead would always be there for me to call home.

"Balance," he'd said, and I didn't argue. Taking a well-deserved rest was something Bastian and I both needed.

So, there I was being escorted through a cute neighborhood, the houses unfamiliar until we stopped. In the living world, Bastian and I had stared at an empty plot of land where this house used to sit. He'd stayed with me while I grieved, while I worked through the awful loss and the blank spot in my memories.

"Do you remember what you said to me in Medusa's lair?" I croaked, not taking my eyes off the house I'd grown up in with its perfectly imperfect blue shudders that Dad and I had painted ourselves, and the slightly off-center birdbath that just would not go together right.

Bastian had asked me to remind him to put a ring on my finger. I'd thought he was joking at the time, but just in case he wasn't, I wanted him to. I wanted him for as long as possible, as long as he would have me.

"I do," he answered, his voice so close as he nudged my ear with his nose. "I've been waiting for you to remind me."

Swallowing thickly, I broke my gaze from my childhood home, and stared at the man I would be with until the end. "This is your reminder."

"Thanks, love, but why don't you take a look at your hand?"

Dumbly, I pulled my eyes from his to stare down at my hand in his. On my third finger was a thick band carved in an exquisite leaf design that spanned from the base of my finger to my knuckle. Resting on top of it was the biggest stone I had ever seen on a ring, the familiar violet color winking at me in the sun.

"How?" I breathed, awestruck.

Bastian chuckled. "It turns out Seph knows a good jeweler." Then he moved, cupping my face in his hands as he tilted my head back. "I want you forever. Will you be mine?"

Instead of responding to a question he already knew the answer to, I pressed up on my toes and kissed him, allowing the joy of this moment to wash through me as I tasted his mouth.

This was where we began, and I couldn't wait to walk into our future together.

Clearing my throat, I lifted my chin, gesturing to the house, a familiar eager bark baying from behind the door. "Care to meet the in-laws?"

"Absolutely," he murmured, bringing my hand to his lips before leading me toward our forever.

THE END

This concludes the Soul Reader Series.
It has been an absolute pleasure sharing Sloane with you.

*If you loved Sloane and want to know more about her sister, Darby, check out the Grave Talker series, starting with **Dead to Me**.*

Are you ready for a new adventure?
Don't miss **Spells & Slip-ups!**
Available for preorder on your favorite retailer!

DEAD TO ME

Grave Talker Book One

Meet Darby. Coffee addict. Homicide detective. Oh, and she can see ghosts, too.

There are only three rules in Darby Adler's life.
One: Don't talk to the dead in front of the living.
Two: Stay off the Arcane Bureau of Investigation's radar.

Three: Don't forget rules one and two.

With a murderer desperate for Darby's attention and an ABI agent in town, things are about to get mighty interesting in Haunted Peak, TN.

Grab Dead to Me today!

SPELLS AND SLIP-UPS

The Wrong Witch Book One

I suck at witchcraft.

Coming from a long line of famous witches, I should be
at the top of the heap. Problem is, if there is a spell cast
anywhere in my vicinity, I will somehow mess it up. As
a probationary agent with the Arcane Bureau of
Investigation, I have two choices: I can limp along and
maybe pass myself off as a competent agent, or I can
fail. *Miserably.*

Worse news? If I can't get my act together, I may not only be out of a job, I could also lose my life.

Whose idea was this again?

Preorder now!
Coming June 7, 2022

THE ROGUE ETHEREAL SERIES

an adult urban fantasy series by Annie Anderson

Enjoy the Soul Reader Series?
Then you'll love Max!

Come meet Max. She's brash. She's inked. She has a bad habit of dying… *a lot.* She's also a Rogue with a demon on her tail and not much backup.
This witch has a serious bone to pick.

Check out the Rogue Ethereal Series today!

THE PHOENIX RISING SERIES

an adult paranormal romance series by Annie Anderson

Heaven, Hell, and everything in between. Fall into the realm of Phoenixes and Wraiths who guard the gates of the beyond. That is, if they can survive that long...

Living forever isn't all it's cracked up to be.

Check out the Phoenix Rising Series today!

JOIN THE LEGION

EXCLUSIVE SNEAK PEEKS,
GIVEAWAYS, BOOK DISCUSSION.
COME FOR THE BOOKS.
STAY FOR THE MEMES.

To stay up to date on all things Annie Anderson, get exclusive access to ARCs and giveaways, and be a member of a fun, positive, drama-free space, join The Legion!

ABOUT THE AUTHOR

 Annie Anderson is the author of the international best-selling Rogue Ethereal series. A United States Air Force veteran, Annie pens fast-paced Urban Fantasy novels filled with strong, snarky heroines and a boatload of magic. When she takes a break from writing, she can be found binge-watching The Magicians, flirting with her husband, wrangling children, or bribing her cantankerous dogs to go on a walk.

To find out more about Annie and her books, visit
www.annieande.com

Made in the USA
Middletown, DE
02 May 2022

65138667R00165